Club Sixxes

ANOTHER CURVY BODY

WENDI ZWADUK

ENTWINED PUBLISHING

Another Curvy Body
ISBN # 978-1-80250-256-5
©Copyright Wendi Zwaduk 2025
Cover Art by Kelly Martin ©Copyright July 2025
Interior text design by Entwined Publishing
Published by Entice, an Entwined Publishing imprint

Published in 2025 by Entwined Publishing, United Kingdom.

Entwined Publishing is a division of Totally Entwined Group Limited.

Club Sixxes
Another Pretty Face
Another Curvy Body

Clandestine Classics
The Phantom of the Opera

Anthologies
Treble: Savin' Me
Boots, Chaps and Cowboy Hats: Between Us

Collections
Naughty or Nice?: Wrapped in Red and Green
Heart Attack: Over My Head
Haunted By You: Miss Me Baby
Wanton Witches: Candlelit Magic
Jolly Rogered: Ruined by the Pirate
Hot Bite: Summer Sizzle
Falsely, Madly, Deeply: From Fake to Forever

ANOTHER CURVY BODY

Dedication

For the Lucky Ducks
For TPS
For KC
For JPZ

Chapter One

I want to be with someone who could love me. Chloe Hunter waited in line at Tracks and patted her watch. When she clubbed, she insisted on wearing the timepiece because it contained her credit card information, her ID and the key to her car. No cards to lose, keys to misplace or purse to carry.

"You here for the dancing or the conversation?" a man behind her asked. He bumped her ass. "Or selling?"

She stepped backward, pretending to trip while intentionally jamming the spiked heel of her shoe into the top of his foot. She glanced back and pasted a ditzy smile on her face. "Sorry! These sidewalks are so uneven." She giggled. "I stepped wrong. Sorry."

"No problem." He winced. "If you're here to dance, then you'd better be careful."

"I'll try to." She kept up the dizzy blonde act. Guys tended to like the facade. She never had understood why. She wanted a partner who accepted her beauty *and* her brains.

"Are you meeting someone here?" he asked.

The heel to the foot wasn't going to get him to leave her alone? Interesting. She clasped her hands together and swept her gaze over him. Not her type at all. Blond men didn't do much for her. Plus, he wasn't much taller than her five-foot-three. She liked tall men. But he did have a boyish charm to him...almost a fake charm. She'd seen a hundred men like him—either trying too hard to be a tough guy or sweet to the point of disarming.

"I'm just here to dance. Not buying or selling or conversation." She shrugged, then turned her attention to the door as the line moved forward. She wished she wasn't to the point of wanting to be with anyone who could love her. She should be with someone who fell hard for her. Wanted her as much as his next breath.

Like that was going to happen.

"I'm meeting my girlfriend," the man offered. "She's here as a bottle girl."

"Oh good." She wasn't sure if this was a lie to make her jealous or if he was showing off. She'd guess the latter. "See you later." She headed up to the bouncer and paid her fee, then went into the club.

The fool behind her, if he was indeed dating a bottle girl, had to know better than to ask if she was there for conversation. The music was too damn loud. Any conversation had to be made at the bar, shouting, or outside on the patio. Even the restrooms were full of pumped-in music.

The bass thumped and people were already jammed into the room. The first time she'd gone clubbing, someone had told her there'd be plenty of space and making connections with people would be easy.

Both were dead wrong.

She noticed the talker from the line dart over to one of the bottle girls and engage her in conversation.

Good luck. She turned her back on him and threaded her way into the crowd. The throb of the bass, the wave of the bodies and the sheer onslaught of sensations were too much. She let herself get caught up in the wave and danced. Nothing else mattered, just existing.

She didn't notice anyone or anything besides the music. The rollicking dance music made her happy. She could be anyone she wanted for a few hours in the club. If someone tried to talk to her, she'd pretend to be an heiress or a street kid. She could be anyone but Chloe, the girl who worked in a law office and had spent the last three years of her life balancing work and taking care of her father.

She wished Darinda had come out tonight. At least she'd have someone to hang out with and not feel so alone. The last she knew, Darinda wasn't into the clubs — or hadn't been until she'd gotten tangled up with the Reid brothers. Lucky girl. Two insanely rich men who wanted nothing but her attention.

Like that would happen to her.

She danced a while longer, then pushed her way to the bar. She waved to the bartender and held up two fingers. The bartender nodded before opening a bottle of water for her.

She tapped her watch to pay for the water and leave a tip, then took two gulps. Dancing gave her release, but it also wore her out. She ducked over to the patio and finished the water.

Coming to the club wasn't going to change her life. It wasn't going to make anything better — except it did. She watched the crowd and wished she wasn't quite so shy. She could dance into the middle of the throng of bodies with no problem and make mild small talk, but letting someone in? That was the impossible part. Guys who came to Tracks weren't interested in a relationship. They wanted a hook-up.

She'd been the good-time girl a few times and it hadn't ever felt right. Why sleep with someone just to leave them the next morning and never see them again? Why put herself out there?

Because she'd never find someone otherwise.

Chloe tossed the bottle in the recycling can, then ducked into the middle of the dancers. She moved to the music again and lost herself in the chaos around her. Some people understood how to dance, but most had no idea. They simply moved. One man caught her attention because he appeared to be throwing elbows — not to hurt anyone. No, he seemed to have no sense of rhythm.

She turned and another man grabbed her attention. This one wasn't anywhere close, but the moment she saw him, she didn't want to look anywhere else.

He caught her gaze and smiled.

Something low in her belly turned to mush. Guys didn't usually have this effect on her. She could be cool and distant. Yes, she might fall in lust with them, but it was always from afar. The instant gut reaction wasn't usual for her.

He sailed through the crowd to her. Although she couldn't understand a word he said because she couldn't hear him above the noise, she allowed him to take her hand. She walked with him to the patio.

"God, it's loud in there." He let go and held the door for her.

"It is." She ducked under his arm, moving out to the patio. Unlike in the club, she could see the various bouncers outside. Inside, the club used a bank of cameras and a few big men for intervention. If this guy bothered her, she'd be protected.

"I saw you in line." He nodded to the bar. "Want a drink?"

"I'm good." She leaned on the fence and crossed her ankles. "You saw me, huh? Where in line?"

"By the door." He laced his fingers together as he leaned his elbow on the fence. "You were being annoyed by the guy behind you."

"You saw that?" She kept her expression blank, so she didn't give away too much interest. The more men thought she was interested, the harder they pushed. If he liked her, even a little bit, then he'd have to work for her affection.

"I did. I know him, too. He's pushy. Wants to hook up with anyone who shows attention." He chuckled. "Did he give you the story about the bottle girl?"

"He did." She eyed him. She'd never seen him at this club. Hadn't seen him anywhere. "You know him?"

"He's an installer. Puts in cabinets and countertops. Nice enough guy, but he's desperate to get laid." He nodded as the female bartender brought him a martini. "Thanks."

"How do you know all that?" She folded her arms. "You just know the backstories of people here?"

"Not exactly." He sipped the drink. "I don't know anything about the bartender. Never met her before."

"Oh." She sighed. "So the installer...what's his story? He's desperate for a date?"

"He's a nice guy, but he's not versed with the fairer sex and tries too hard. He came on to a friend of mine and didn't take it well when she turned him down."

"Friend?" Codeword, *girlfriend*. "I see."

"I doubt you do." He sipped more of the drink. "He's a friend and so is she, but I don't want to date her. Never have."

Another man joined them and her mouth watered. Where the man speaking to her was sexy, this one practically oozed sex appeal as well. Both exuded power. Tall, dark, handsome, soft spoken and not pushy. At least not yet.

She suppressed a shiver. "Hi."

"Hi." The second man crooked his brow. "I see you've met Justin. I'm Martin."

She accepted his hand when he stuck it out and shook hands with Martin. She hadn't gotten around to asking Justin his name. "It's nice to meet you, Martin. Justin has been entertaining me for the last few minutes." She turned her attention to Justin. "It's nice to meet you, too."

"Martin would've busted my balls, but I forget my manners and to introduce myself." He left his half-empty glass on the table in front of them. "Forgive me."

"You're forgiven." She snorted. She wasn't sure what he played at, but if he wanted her attention, he had it. "Why are you talking to me?"

"Huh?" Martin inclined his head. "Why wouldn't we?"

"I'm not out there shaking my ass all over everywhere, not letting my boobs hang out, not throwing myself at you. There are fifty others in there who'd do that." She had a tendency of talking herself out of things she deserved. "Sorry."

"You don't have to be sorry." Justin stood tall and hooked his fingers in his pockets. "You're right. There are others who would throw themselves in our direction."

"But I'm not?" she asked.

"You're beautiful and caught my attention," Justin replied. "I wanted to talk to you. Get to know you."

"Is that bad?" Martin asked. "It's not like you can have a conversation in the club. Jesus, you can't hear a nuclear explosion in there."

An odd turn of phrase, but true. "Sorry."

"You've been hurt, haven't you?" Justin asked. "Been jerked around in there?"

She shrugged to disguise her frustration. So she had been jerked around, as they put it. So what? She'd been used a few times in there, too. She didn't feel like she belonged. But what was new?

"I'd take you to the VIP section, but it's not any quieter there. It's better out here," Martin said. "Would you like a drink?"

"No, thank you." She liked to keep her wits about her. "How about a dance?"

"Out here?" Martin's eyes flashed.

The predatory look did something for her. The twinge in her belly? No. The shiver up her spine? Not quite. Her pussy thrum? Yes. He made her wet with that glance. She turned her attention to Justin. He created the same reaction within her. She wanted to shimmy between them and feel both men touch her.

"Come on," she said and grasped each man's hand. "I like this song." She led them back into the main room of the club just beyond the edge of the dancers. The position gave her plenty of room to be with them, but also the opportunity to disappear if they got too grabby. She positioned herself between them.

Martin tucked in behind her, rubbing her ass along his groin. He slid his hands over her hips. He brushed his lips across her bare shoulder.

She bit back a groan and thanked God she'd decided to wear a strappy dress tonight. She loved when her partner kissed her shoulders and the back of her neck.

Justin fitted against her, chest to chest and groin to groin. She draped her arms around his neck. His smile warmed her to her core. She swayed with him and Martin as one body moving to the beat of the music. Justin nuzzled her jaw. She gazed into his eyes and her breath was wrenched from her body. She loved men with brown eyes. When she stared into his eyes, so deep and dark she could get lost in them, she whimpered. She longed to straddle his thigh and ride him.

She moaned. Being between them, caged, but also protected, excited her. She loved the way they touched her. Together, the tenderness and sweetness were more than she could handle. She tipped her head back and rested it against Martin's shoulder. When Justin palmed her breast, she cried out—not that anyone could hear her. She snapped her eyes open and parted her lips. He hadn't pinched or grabbed. A simple sensual caress. Her nipple beaded beneath his fingertips. She loved the instant reaction to him and the way he made fire surge through her veins. She gasped.

Justin let go and turned her around, allowing her to face Martin. He had the same dark eyes, but a few more lines around those eyes. Where Justin was almost baby-faced, Martin was a bit more weathered. He smiled and her knees weakened. She rubbed her nose along his. Part of her wanted to strip naked and give herself over to him.

To them.

Justin grinded behind her, but it wasn't lascivious. More like one of the most sensual things she'd ever done in her life. He moved with reverence. Touched her like she mattered.

Martin trailed his fingers along her arm, then kissed her. She'd imagined his lips would be soft, but she hadn't expected the connection to be that intoxicating. She opened to him immediately and sucked on his tongue. The man was like velvet. She groaned into the kiss. He threaded his fingers into her hair and held her close while Justin caressed her from behind.

She barely heard the music and the crowd was non-existent. Nothing else mattered except being between these two men. She danced and luxuriated in their attention. For once, she felt important, but also cherished and desired.

She broke the kiss and continued to dance with them. Martin swayed with her and grinned. His toothy smile hinted at a boyishness he probably hid. She wasn't sure what he might do for a living. His dress and demeanor didn't give away his profession.

Right now, she didn't care.

As she danced, she slid her hand over Justin's cheek. Touching him sent electrical sparks through her system. The same thing happened when she rubbed against Martin. She'd never been attracted to two men at once. She tended to be a one-man woman. But being between them made her rethink her choices.

Her wrist vibrated and she checked the message on her watch. A text. *Shit.*

Come home. Madelin ran away.

She groaned. Her sister Melinda didn't understand her own daughter, Madelin, and expected Madelin to simply go along with her mother's wishes. Chloe wasn't a parent, but she'd taken care of her father for the last three years until the cancer won. Some days she wasn't sure how she'd made it to twenty-eight with her wits intact. The one thing she did know was that the more Melinda pushed Madelin, the more Madelin separated from the family. She also knew what'd happened to Madelin, though. The young woman had run away and most likely, Chloe knew where she'd gone.

She disengaged from both men and wished she didn't have to leave.

Before she got too far, Martin grasped her fingers. He tipped his head. She pointed to the patio.

Justin and Martin followed her to the relatively quiet space.

"I need to go," she said. "Long story short, my niece ran away and she's probably at my apartment. I can't leave a fourteen year old alone at this hour of the night."

"Is she your problem?" Justin asked. "Your custody?"

"No." She shook her head. "She feels safe with me."

"You're the closest thing to a parent she's got?" Martin asked.

"More like she's a tomboy and is still coming into her own, but she's not the girly girl her mother wants. Instead of letting her find her own path, she's being pushed." She shrugged and checked her watch for another message. Thankfully, there wasn't one. "Look, I need to go. I had a great time, but this faerie princess has to go back to her regular life. Thanks for a wonderful evening. I'll never forget you." She ducked under Justin's arm and rushed into the building. She didn't bother to look back until she stood out in the parking garage next to the club. Even then, she didn't stop moving until she reached her car.

Once she slid behind the wheel, she locked the vehicle and engaged the engine. She'd learned so many things, living on her own. Never stay still for long and never be in any area where it wasn't secure. She backed out of the spot and headed home.

She should've gotten Justin's or Martin's phone number. Should've been nicer about leaving.

Damn her sense of family and responsibility.

She'd lose out on something great because she had to help those she loved and those who drove her to the brink of insanity. Madelin needed her help.

This night would have to live in her memory.

So much for trying to find a date.

Chapter Two

Justin Cooper stared at the spot where she'd been. He didn't even know her name, but she'd captivated him. The space she'd taken up was soon swallowed by other dancers. Martin elbowed him, the silent gesture a signal to leave the dance floor.

As he moved through the people, his mind wandered. He might be at the club, but mentally, he was a million miles away. She'd just left. Walked away, not even a glance back, and disappeared.

The whole thing seemed impossible.

A woman danced up to him at the perimeter of the crowd. She rubbed on him and grasped his hand. Unlike his mystery girl who created instant sparks within him, this woman didn't have that effect. She barely registered to him. He smiled, careful not to be mean, shook his head and kept going.

She'd probably be upset, but he didn't care. He wasn't at the club to snag a girlfriend. Hell, he'd learned that years ago. Clubs were great for dancing, losing oneself for a few hours and drinking. Lots of drinking.

But conversation? No.

He'd hooked up a few times, but nothing lasting. How could he have something meant to go the distance when they barely exchanged names and were simply two bodies moving in the darkness?

Besides, he wasn't Martin. He'd never been married. He snorted. Forty-two years old and he'd never been married. Barely had long-term girlfriends. He didn't want to be tied down.

Martin kept up with him and joined him in the parking garage in the valet line. "What was that all about?"

"What was what?" He gestured to the valet. "She left."

"I know she did, but there was another one." Martin stuffed his hands into his pockets. "She was cute."

"The first one was cuter."

"I agree. She was one in a million." Martin stared at him, his expression blank. "What are you thinking? She walked away."

"I'm thinking we should find her." Like right now. He gritted his teeth as he waited for the driver to show up. *Where the fuck is Paul?* He only trusted one driver with their favorite sports car.

"Whoa." Martin nodded to the approaching car. "Let's discuss this in private."

He agreed and waited until they were in the luxury vehicle. He paid the valet before driving off. "What do you mean, let's discuss? I'm listening." Barely. Seething was more like it. How could she just drive off? Women didn't do that to him.

"She left, and of course she did." Martin rested his arm on the sill. "She fit our bill pretty well and never gave us her name. Don't you think that's odd?"

"I did." He'd wanted her name, but there wasn't much time to ask for it. "You don't like that?"

"I'm not sure."

"She seemed to like us."

"She did."

He turned into the main flow of traffic and sped toward their home. "She practically melted in our embrace. We should've demanded her name. Demanded she let us take her home. Should've shown her we're not playing games."

"And alienate her?" Martin sighed and drummed his fingers on the sill. "Besides, where were we going to put her?"

He had to concede on that point. The two-seater vehicle wasn't exactly suitable for giving a third person a ride. "Fine."

"She's a sweet girl, but she might not be interested in something with us. She might not even want something long-term. What if she's not interested in what we do?"

"Contracting? We barely touch that any longer." He kept up with the flow of traffic.

"Not that," Martin grumbled. "I meant what we do in the bedroom. What if she can't handle both of us? What if she's not interested in both? She might be a one-man kind of woman. She might not want to share anyone in the bedroom."

Fuck. He hadn't thought of all that. He'd thought about how well she fit between them. How much he liked the way she tasted. The way she sighed against him. The way she hadn't seemed to be turned off by both men touching her. "She should want to be with us."

"Should."

"What's there to dislike? We're two rich bachelors. We're single, stable and trying to mingle with her. We'd give her the moon and the stars if she'd give us the chance." He turned onto the side street leading to their home.

"We're seen as a catch."

Martin's blunt statement bothered him. "Right…"

"Except us being a catch isn't a good thing. There will always be someone who wants to be with us because they want to advance themselves. Do you want a woman who will lie to you? Who will use you for money?"

He winced, but tried to hide his reaction. His brother knew all too well about being used. Cindy had been the love of his life, but she hadn't loved Justin and hadn't wanted to be in a throuple. When she'd died in that crash, he thought he'd lost everything. He'd never been able to forgive himself for being so angry with Martin for marrying someone who didn't want them both. Then Molly showed up. She seemed to like them both, but Martin refused to get serious. Justin hadn't known why—until he checked his accounts. She'd made withdrawals on the business account, paying herself.

Molly might have liked them both, but she liked their money more.

"I loved Cindy, but she wasn't what we needed. She had my heart," Martin said. "Molly was cute, but she had a tough core and again, wasn't what we needed."

He pulled into the long driveway leading back to their mansion. As the wheels moved silently on the concrete, he mulled over what Martin had said. There were a lot of people in the world wanting to do others harm. A lot of women would see him and his cousin as a means to a financial end.

"We could run into the same thing with this woman," Martin said. "What if she turns out to be just another person looking for a paycheck?"

"I don't think she's like that." He parked in the garage. "We've had our pictures plastered all over everywhere. We're not low-profile people. She has to know who the hell we are and if she wanted money, then she should've been begging for drinks. Should've been trying to get into the VIP area. Any chance to get something. She barely even spent time with us on the dance floor. We talked longer out on the patio where she wouldn't be seen."

"True." He stopped the engine, then closed the garage door. The light flooded the space. "You want me to stop."

"I think you're getting ahead of yourself." Martin left the vehicle and stood. "But I never said you should stop."

Good. He hadn't wanted to hear that anyway. "Then what?"

"We need to be patient," Martin said. "Give it time. If she's meant to come back into our lives — which I think she is — then she will. She found us by chance, I'm convinced, and there's a good chance she'll find us again. I don't even believe that this was finding because of our station. I can't shake the feeling this was all a coincidence. I can't say if she'll be interested in being with both of us. She might not. Two men in bed is a lot to handle."

He leaned on the roof of the car. "You really feel that way?"

"I do."

He trusted his cousin's gut instincts. Martin had a better idea of what to do and was more analytical.

Justin tended to follow his heart. Good for design, but terrible for pragmatism.

"She wasn't looking for us. Hell, she seemed shocked by our names. Not excited shock or conniving shock, but genuine surprise. I didn't get the feeling she knew who we are."

"I didn't," he said. He hadn't trusted his guts, though. Being with her felt like being himself. He didn't have to put on airs or peacock for her. Just be Justin Cooper, the creative, free-spirited guy who liked to dance and have a good time. He and his cousin were just Martin and Justin, not the famous Cooper cousins.

"Then don't worry about it. We'll find her. We don't have to go looking for her, but if the fairy tale is right, things will come back around," Martin said. "I don't like fairy tales, but they do come true sometimes, don't they?"

"They do." He had to agree. He followed his cousin into the house. "I just wish we'd learned her name."

"There's a chance we can." Martin sat at the bar and fiddled with his phone. "Being VIPs at the club does have some perks."

"What?" He joined his cousin at the bar. "What are you doing?"

"Sin, the head bouncer, has a record of everyone who comes in. They've got video and since he worked the door tonight, he might know who she is." He tapped the phone. "I just texted him and he could get back to me."

"Could?" His cousin had always been the brains of their company, but this made little sense.

"Sin told me he wanted some work done on his bathroom. I might have said he could get priority if he helped us out."

"You're terrible."

"You know it." Martin abandoned the phone. "Look, we found a woman who made us both reconsider being bachelors for the remainder of our life. I'm not saying she's the one. She might not be, but why not try to reconnect with her in a totally non-stalker way? I saw how Nathan and Nick Reid orchestrated the beginning of the relationship with Darinda. She wasn't keen on being pursued that way, or being pushed, and I don't blame her. This one might not want that kind of pushing, either."

"I guess not." He wasn't fond of being that conniving. He wanted someone to fall in love with him because of him, not because of cash, position in society or something like that.

"I don't want to orchestrate this. Just get an idea of who she is. If we can do a background check on her, find out if she's the kind of girl we want to be with, then we do. It's no different than finding out if a potential employee is a good fit." Martin kicked out of his shoes. "I want another love like I had with Cindy. Is it possible? I don't know. I never thought lightning could strike twice, but I've learned not to rule anything out."

"I know." He nodded his head and stuffed his hands into his pockets. "I've never said anything, but I've been jealous of you."

Martin snapped his attention to Justin. "What? How?"

He hadn't planned on talking about this, but now that he'd opened the door, he couldn't shut it. "The relationship you had with Cindy. When I saw you two together, I knew that was love. Knew that was something to go the distance."

"She wasn't fond of you. Not like that."

"But I accepted it. I never pressed her to be with the both of us. I saw her with you and you both suited each other. There wasn't room for me." He leaned against the bar, resting his back into the granite. "I didn't have a place there, but I wanted that kind of love. I'm dying to be wanted in the way she wanted you."

"You've had all those women. None of them brought that out?" Martin abandoned his wallet and keys on the counter, then unhooked his belt. "What about…?"

"I can have lots of dates, but not really connect with them." He shrugged. "And you can't name a woman I might have connected that way with because there wasn't one. I never brought any around."

Martin slowly shook his head. "I guess you didn't."

"Didn't you ever wonder why I never had a girlfriend at Christmas festivities?" he asked. "Family reunions?"

"I just assumed you were between relationships." Martin frowned, then chuckled and sank onto the stool. "Why didn't you ever bring anyone around?"

"Besides the fact that your mother would've killed me for not letting her background check the woman first, I never had anyone that ever seemed to match the intensity and love that you shared with Cindy. Why subject a woman to the circus that was our family when I knew she wasn't going to hang around? Uncle Les and his musings on politics, Granny and her incessant need to have everyone cook with her, Uncle Lloyd discussing the various things he'd eaten over the course of his life, Aunt Marnie wanting to plan everyone's weddings…if it wasn't overwhelming enough, then throw a woman who won't stick around because it's too much to handle. No, not doing that."

"Can't say I blame you."

"You and I always had that connection. We did things together. Until Cindy, we were that twosome who shared. I tried to find someone who could be my version of Cindy, but she never showed." He gritted his teeth. He might be a dreamer and creative, but he hated to be emotional.

"She will." Martin nodded once. "She's out there."

"The one that makes all three of us whole?"

"I'm sure of it."

He hoped Martin was right. He'd waited too long to find someone and didn't want to be alone any longer.

"I'm heading to bed. I've got contracts to look over and to speak with Sheldon about the kitchen reno over in Grove City. Are you going to work on those drawings for the Napier place?"

"Already done." He clapped Martin on the back. "Go. I'll be okay."

"I worry about you."

"I worry about me, too." He left his phone and wallet with Martin's on the counter. "But I'm a survivor, like you. We'll be okay."

Martin dipped his head once more, then left Justin alone in the kitchen.

Justin sighed and massaged his temples. *Christ.* He wasn't one to get caught up on a woman like this. He dated and enjoyed the ladies, but he didn't have ties. Hadn't ever wanted them as he did now. His mystery girl might not want them, either. She might want to play the field or simply be free.

Why was he caught up on her?

When he looked into her eyes, he saw forever. The cool green attracted him. Then there was her smile. God, she warmed him to his core. He loved the way she tasted and how she opened to him without a second thought. She hadn't talked to them for long, but she gave every impression she wasn't going to put up with much.

He closed his eyes for a moment and let his memory run back to the dance with her. He loved women with curves and she had the right ones in places women should be curvy. She had just enough ass to grind into him and knew how to touch him, too. He longed for her kiss again. Longed to hold her.

A buzzing sound ripped him from his thoughts. He opened his eyes and sought out the noise. He spotted his cousin's phone lit up.

He and Martin had no secrets from each other and tended to answer the other's phones when busy. One of his favorite things to do was answer Martin's phone, playing along until the person on the other end realized it was him and not Martin. He swiped to check why the phone was buzzing.

A text.

He retrieved the message from Sin.

Her name is Chloe Hunter. 28. Likes to dance. Doesn't cause trouble.

He thanked Sin for the information and said he'd speak to him in the morning. After he'd sent the text, he brought the phone to his cousin. "Marty?"

"Yeah?" Martin shouted.

When he cracked the door open, he heard the shower. He should've guessed. Justin ventured into the room and stood at the entrance to the bathroom. "You got a text from Sin. About our girl."

"Oh?" The water shut off and Martin's voice became clearer. "And?"

"Chloe Hunter. Twenty-eight. Didn't say more, other than she's a dancer and good egg." He left the phone on the dresser. "I let him know you'd contact him in the morning."

"Thanks." Martin strode out of the bathroom, wrapped only in a towel. "Appreciate it."

"So?" He leaned on the dresser. "Are you going to check her out?"

Martin grinned. "You know I will."

He nodded, glad his cousin was the brains. "Thanks."

"We have a name and can figure out if she's someone we should approach. Like I said, she came into our orbit for a reason and she'll be back. Now we have a bit of a leg up, too." Martin's grin widened. "I like her, too. I want another dance with her, so if there's a possibility, we're taking it."

"Good." He preferred when he and Martin were on the same page. "Get some rest."

"I will. You, too." Martin paused. "Soon we'll have this all figured out and can be the family we all deserve."

He nodded, then left the room. The family they deserved…what a nice concept. He couldn't remember the last time he'd had an actual family outside of Martin. He ducked into his bedroom and kept the lights off.

Darkness settled around him and he embraced the quiet. He needed to calm his mind and rest. He'd found someone he wanted and had to work with Martin to figure out how to find her. Now that he and Martin realized they needed to share their partner and didn't have forever to find her, he wanted to act so they could have the family they deserved.

Have a future.

Have love.

All easier said than done.

Chapter Three

Chloe clocked into work and settled at her desk. She missed having Darinda there, but she liked the better cubicle. At least over here she could see the outside and feel the sunshine. She clicked through the various documents in her queue and made a note of how she wanted to tackle the list of tasks.

She hadn't been back to the club in a week. Part of her told herself it was because she wasn't in the mood to dance, but the rest of her knew the truth. She worried she'd run into Martin and Justin again.

Her hands trembled as she thought about them. Martin and Justin were men way out of her league. Handsome, classy, and they'd seemed to listen to her.

A lethal combination.

But she'd run away. Most guys didn't want a woman who escaped. But she'd had to take care of Madelin. Her phone buzzed and she checked the notification.

A text from Madelin.

Made it to practice. Will text when I head home.

She replied with a *thanks* after she got the photo of Madelin at band camp. She massaged her temples and sighed. Madelin wasn't a bad kid. She simply needed a place to belong. Hopefully, she'd get things sorted out with her parents, but until then she had a room with her.

She turned her attention back to her work and sorted through the documents.

"Hey." Darinda rushed up to her and sat beside her on one of the other office chairs. "I finally got five minutes to come out here."

She abandoned her work and gave her friend her full attention. "Hi." She sagged in her seat. "I miss our daily chats. How are you?"

"I know. I got my promotion and things went to shit with my friends," Darinda said. "I'm okay. You?"

"You got promoted to the fiancée of the bosses. How could you not be okay?" She laughed and grasped Darinda's hand. "I mean, a double diamond ring? You're so lucky."

"They spoil me." Darinda frowned. "How's your niece?"

"Madelin? She's good. She's starting to figure out who she is and slowly finding that she likes makeup. She'll never be a frilly girl," she said. "But that's okay. I'm not a frilly girl."

"Don't have to be."

She swept her gaze over Darinda. Her friend looked so happy. Practically glowing. "Do you have a little bit to talk?"

"Always." Darinda leaned forward. "What's wrong? You look stressed."

"Not so much stressed, but I need to talk to someone."

"Then let's go down to the coffee shop and talk." Darinda grabbed her hand and yanked her to her feet. Within a few moments, she and Darinda were down in what had once been called the cafeteria, but had been transformed into a series of shops—coffee, sandwich, Asian and Latin cuisines. The space felt more like a little street and the atmosphere was much calmer. She joined Darinda at one of the smaller tables.

"Want something to drink?" Darinda pulled out her phone. "I get a slight advantage. They'll bring it to me."

"Well...can I have a latte?" She didn't want to be seen taking advantage of Darinda's perks or for Darinda to think she'd been friends with her for said perks, but if she had the chance, why not take it?

"You bet." Darinda fiddled with her phone a moment, then put the device down. "Okay, so talk. What's wrong? I don't like seeing you all crinkled up."

"I'm crinkled?" She hadn't noticed.

"You usually walk through here with your head up and your eyes bright. You look like you've got the weight of the world on your shoulders," Darinda said. "Talk to me."

God. Now that she had the chance to talk, the words wouldn't come. She scrubbed her forehead with the back of her hand. "I met these guys."

"Ooh!" Darinda scooted closer. "Cute? Handsome?"

"Let me back up. My older sister feels she can't control Madelin and Mad ran away to my apartment. I don't mind—it's nice to have the company—but she's not a bad kid. She's not even rotten. She's just misunderstood and living with a helicopter parent. I think she's trying to contact her birth father, which will cause a whole host of other problems, but they're not mine to solve."

"That's a lot to handle," Darinda said. "You really do have a lot on your shoulders."

"I'll manage, but in the midst of all this, I met two guys." She balled her hands to hide the trembling. "Justin and Martin. They're handsome, refined and I don't know much else about them."

"That's not totally horrible."

"No, but I don't even know if I deserve them."

"Do you have to choose between them? You know you don't have to choose, right?" Darinda asked. "I mean, I don't know if you're that open-minded, but there's a lot of fun to be had with two men."

"You should know." She wasn't jealous of Darinda. In awe, maybe, but not jealous.

"I do, but it's more than that. Two men who are totally devoted to you and want nothing but to make you happy. It's like being a princess all the time," Darinda said. "It's not for everyone, but it might be something you'd like."

"Maybe." She picked at the simple silver ring she wore on her middle finger. "There are things about me they don't know and maybe not both of them want me."

"Who wouldn't want you?"

She rolled her eyes. Plenty of men didn't want her. She hesitated before speaking again. She'd rather talk about her sex life with her partner, not her friend. "I'm not…tame in the bedroom."

"No?" Darinda reached across the table. "Honey, there's nothing wrong with being not tame."

"No?"

Darinda held on to her hand and scooted around the table, extra close. "I'm not tame, either."

"No?" She hadn't expected Darinda to say that. "What?"

"Did you think I was mousy?"

"No." But she hadn't thought Darina might be into kink.

"Let me ask you this. What's your poison? Mine is not only two men—two men in particular—but also bondage. I like being tied up, like being spanked, like being shown off, like to watch and I love toys."

She needed a second to process what Darinda had said, but she also liked having a kindred spirit. "Wow."

"You're put off?"

"No." She squeezed Darinda's hand. "God, no. We're on a lot of the same wavelengths. I don't know about being with two men because I've never done that, but the rest...yes." She nodded. Darinda understood. Finally, someone got it. "I'm not alone."

"Nope, not alone."

"It's good to know." She hugged Darinda. "I don't know if these guys are even into this or if they want to share me. I don't know."

"Who says you need to know? You just met them." Darinda winked as the coffees were delivered. "But I also know what you can do so you can explore what you might like and figure out if you're interested in other things." She waited for the server to leave before she spoke again. "You know?"

At least she could understand what Darinda was getting at. "I do."

"I recommend Club Sixxes. I can get you in and you can play there a few times to decide if it's what you like. Yeah? If there's a kink there, you can try it."

She almost fell out of her chair. "You're kidding."

"Nope."

She wobbled and forgot about her surroundings for a few moments. "Yes. I want to go there. I want to explore." *I want to be free to be myself.* She couldn't say that out loud. "I'm interested."

Darinda grinned, then let go long enough to sip her drink. "I'll get you hooked up."

"I don't deserve it, but thank you." She held the cup, but didn't otherwise move it on the table. "How...how did you know to go there? I tried to get in, but I didn't get my membership approved."

Darinda sipped the drink again. "To be honest, I love to club. Strike that. Make it past tense. I *loved* to club. I'd go to Tracks, Sixxes and other clubs to escape. Not be me for a while. When I'd go to Sixxes, for example, I could dance, dress sexily and have a good time. Then I discovered the other things happening there and decided, yeah, I want to do that, too. I had a friend who's a Dom and he used to show me off. I loved every second. I found out what I liked, what I didn't and where my limits were. It was a good exploration."

"Wow." She'd thought she was the only one who knew about the club. "That's..."

"Shocking? Gross?" Darinda sighed and pushed her drink away. "It's not for everyone."

"No." She held up her hand. "Stop. Wanting to be free and have a good time is never bad. You were trying to figure out what you wanted and who you are. That's so worth it."

"Oh."

"The reason I couldn't finish my sentence was...I thought I was the only one. I thought no one else understood. I mean, we never talked about this stuff, but I wanted to tell you about the things I did. I wanted someone to tell me I'm not the only one and I'm not a freak."

"You're certainly not that." Darinda's shoulders sagged and she grinned. "Promise."

"I don't get to go to the dance clubs often, but I go for the same reason. I just want to be anyone but the nobody in the office. We're all interchangeable here." She hated to say that, but it was the truth.

"We're not. I get it, though. We all have these little spots in the office and it seems like no one sees us, but they do. I bet you're noticed more than you realize," Darinda said. "But go to Sixxes. I'll make sure you've got a pass by the end of the day so you could even go tonight."

"Really?"

"Sure." Darinda slid her cup back toward her. "Give it a chance and see if you like it. You might meet someone there. Maybe even the guys."

She sighed, but finally took a drink from her latte. "I couldn't get that lucky."

Darinda shrugged and tapped her cup on the table. "To be honest, six months ago, I'd have agreed wholeheartedly. I mean, I felt like you, like I didn't belong. Then things happened. I don't know how they happened or why the guys ended up in my orbit, but I'm glad they did." She paused. "No, I know how they did. They'd been keeping tabs on me and made a move. Maybe Justin and...Martin? Maybe they'll do the same thing."

"I doubt it." They didn't strike her as anyone who'd do that. "They seemed pretty regular."

"What's regular?" Darinda stood. "I need to get you back to work before I get in trouble."

She stood and pushed in her chair, then lowered her voice. "You'll like getting in trouble. You'll get a good spanking for it."

"You know it." Darinda laughed and elbowed her. "And I love every second."

"I know you will." She would. She'd love to be the one on display and getting her ass spanked red. She shivered. Would Justin and Martin do that? Would they be turned on? Or repulsed? She'd never know if she didn't ask. She'd also never know if she never ran into them again.

"I'll text you that code and how to use it, okay?" Darinda walked with her. "Don't toss that. Take it to your desk. You deserve it and it shouldn't get wasted."

"You bet." She one-arm hugged her friend, then paused in the hallway. "Thank you."

"Thank you. You have no idea how much talking to you over the last year helped. It made me feel less alone." Darinda winked. "So thank you for that."

"You're welcome." She waited another second and watched Darinda leave, then headed to her desk. She shook her head, but the smile never left her lips. She wasn't alone. Wasn't the only one liking the things she did and going the places she went.

She settled in her chair and set to work. The faster she got caught up, the faster she'd be done. Hopefully, she'd have time to visit Sixxes tonight. Maybe she'd finally get her membership approved.

She snorted. No one wanted to know about her growing up out in the cornfields.

Two hours later, she finished the last of the backed-up files. As a reward, she checked her phone. Madelin had gotten home. She texted Mad, making sure she had a good time at practice, then switched to her browser and shopped for something to wear to the club. If she was going to a swanky place, then she wanted to look the part.

She found a couple of bondage dresses that caught her attention. Sexy enough to garner attention, but not too revealing that she'd have to explain her attire to anyone. Besides, the unseasonable chilly August weather meant she could get away with a coat over the dress. She checked the availability, then placed an order. She'd pick up the garment on her way home.

A moment later, her phone buzzed with an incoming text from Darinda.

Here's the code. Use it on the website and it'll get you three months' membership. Enjoy and have a kinky time!

She clutched the phone and bit back a whimper. She replied in seconds.

Thank you! I will!

She laughed to herself, then stifled the noise. No one else needed to know what she was doing. She'd go to the club tonight and have a ball. A painful, exhilarating sexy ball.

* * * *

Chloe smoothed her dress and stood in the foyer of the club. She'd never been to Sixxes, but had thoroughly investigated the establishment through the website. Latex wasn't her ideal for a garment, but the dress made her feel not only sexy, but free. No one cared if she looked good or had too many curves. They simply saw her.

She pulled the code up on her phone and waited for the doorman to gesture for her.

"Miss Hunter?" The doorman held up the scanner. "Good to meet you, I'm Danny. I see you've already passed the background check. You've also got a sponsor in Mr. Reid. Quite the endorsement."

Mr. Reid? Must've been Darinda, through Nick or Nathan's account, but still. She'd nabbed quite the help. "Thank you."

"This way. I'd like you to talk to Denise. She's in induction." He gestured to a small room just inside the doorway to the right.

A woman with jet black hair and the tightest corset she'd ever seen sat behind a wrought iron desk. She smiled. "Come in. We've been expecting you."

"Oh." She inched into the room and jerked when the door closed. "I'm being inducted?" She'd had her membership approved?

"Yes. I'm Denise and I'm in induction. Feel free to ask questions," Denise said. "Now, there are a few rules. You may play and get involved as you wish, but do know there are contracts involved with many of the players. Many may not want an interloper without permission. Do ask before joining."

"I understand." She wasn't sure if she should be saying that, but it seemed logical.

"Also, you have a safe word. Use it. We respect each other here and if you feel you need to use it, then do. The idea is to have fun, but if you feel something other than fun has happened, please let me know."

"Does that happen often?" Chloe asked. "People not having fun?"

"Not often, no. Everyone should be free to play as they choose, but some do act out of kind and we need to know. There are additional rules, but they're posted and you're expected to read them. The biggest rule is to report if you see something out of sorts, but what happens in the club stays in the club. We don't advertise for a reason. Understood?"

"I do." She placed her phone in her purse and offered both the purse and her keys to the doorman. "Thank you."

"Welcome." He accepted the items. "You're number thirty-six, but if you forget, I've got you entered into the computer. Enjoy your night and I hope it's beyond your wildest, sexiest dreams."

"Thank you." She sucked in a ragged breath and headed into the playroom. She wasn't sure what to expect in this club. Each establishment was different, but offered many of the same options for play. The deep red walls and thick dark carpet added a bit of warmth to the space. The lighting kept the focus on each play space, rather than the entirety of the room. She noticed a woman cuffed to a St. Andrew's cross. A man encased in latex brandished the crop, spanking her red. Another woman perched on her hands and knees on a bondage bed. Neither woman wore a stitch of clothing. The woman on the bench cried out as a man in black trousers spanked her with his bare hands.

A couple cried out from the round bed under another spotlight. The woman rode the man, her breasts bouncing and the clips on her nipples sparkling in the light.

Her own nipples beaded in anticipation. Her pussy heated and she pressed her knees together. She wanted to jump into the fray, but the rules were not to join without permission.

She swept her gaze across the room again and noticed two men in all black, watching the various scenes from a couch. She knew them. Didn't she? She inched closer and her breath lodged in her throat.

Martin and Justin.

Holy fuck.

If she could play with anyone there, she wanted to play with them. Would they let her? *Only one way to find out.*

She forced herself to move and approached them. "Sirs." She bowed her head and clasped her hands behind her back. "Funny seeing you here. May I sit with you? Before you?"

Dear God. Just let them allow her to join them. Just for a little while.

Chapter Four

Martin kept a bland expression on his face, but inwardly he jumped for joy. Thank fuck Darinda had tipped him off to Chloe's visit. He and Justin had caught up to Chloe. Seeing her tonight in that dress not only made him hard as hell, it made him want to spirit her from the club. He held out his hand. "Join us."

Justin moved aside, creating room between them. "Please, do."

She perched in the gap and shifted her gaze from him to Justin. "I never thought I'd see you here."

"No?" Justin asked. "Is that good? Or bad?"

Ah, his cousin tended to ask too many questions. He simply swept his gaze over her, taking in the beauty. His mouth watered. He longed to run his hands along her body and remove that dress. If he had his way, he'd have her naked between them.

"It's a good thing you're here, but I thought I'd ruined my chance to see you." She turned her attention to Martin. "I ran out so fast."

"That happens." He curled his fingers under her chin, keeping her gaze his direction. "You're worth waiting for."

"I am?"

"Very much so." Justin trailed his fingers along her bare arms. "You're here. I assume you want to play?"

She shivered and parted her lips. Her lashes fluttered and a bit of blush infused her cheeks. She leaned into Martin. "I'd love to play. May I play with you?"

"Do you want to watch awhile first?" Martin asked. "There's quite the show tonight."

Her breathing increased and she slid her hand over his thigh. "Not sure what I want to do."

Interesting. Martin caressed her bottom lip and debated what he wanted to do with her.

Justin kissed her shoulder, then eased his arms around her waist. "How about we go into one of the private rooms and negotiate? We could turn on a movie or use one of the rooms with a viewing window, then figure it out from there."

She gasped and brushed her hand over the bulge in Martin's trousers. "I'd love that." She leaned into him. Her breath tickled his cheeks. "Please? I want to submit to you."

Then he wouldn't let her down. Martin produced a chain collar from his pocket. He hadn't been sure she'd show up or if she'd even be inclined to play, but damn it, he wasn't allowing her to go off with someone else, unless that someone was Justin. Too many other men there would love to play with her, but he doubted they'd be as reverential.

"Oh…" She nodded. "May I wear that? For you?"

"One requirement," Martin said and opened the clasp on the chain. "If you're submitting to me, you're submitting to Justin as well."

"Yes, sirs." She nodded slightly. "I want to."

"The other requirement," Justin said. "Tell us your name, babe."

She froze, then her eyes widened. "I never told you."

"No, you didn't," Martin murmured. "Will you tell us?" Not that he didn't already know. There wasn't much she could disclose now, but that wasn't important.

"Chloe Hunter." She brushed her cheek on his hand. "May we go into a private room?"

"We can now." Justin rose to his feet first and offered his hand.

When she stood, Martin jumped up behind her and slid the collar around her throat. Fuck, the platinum chain looked shiny against her skin. Before she could put her hair back into place, he kissed the back of her neck. She leaned into him and sighed.

She'd be so much fun as a partner.

With Justin in the lead, Martin caged her between them and walked with his cousin to the back of the room where the corridor led to the private rooms. In this case, he didn't mind Justin leading. He needed to be sure no one else stepped in on their prize. They'd found her and he wasn't about to let her slip away so easily.

Once in the private space, he closed the door. Martin gestured to the sofa. "Have a seat."

"Yes, sirs." She settled on the floor at Justin's feet.

"No." Justin patted the cushion. "Up here. The scene hasn't started yet."

"We need to negotiate and talk a bit first," Martin said and sat across from them on the bondage bed. He wanted to be able to look at her when they all talked. "You're here. What brought you here?"

"A friend told me to give this place a try." She folded her hands on her lap. "I've been to other clubs and I like to play, but I wasn't sure how to get in here, or if I'd even belong."

"I see." Justin slid his arm around her shoulders. "What were you looking for when you came here?"

She squeezed her fingers, but didn't reply.

"What he means is, what are your kinks, babe?" Martin rested his elbows on his knees and reached for her.

She grasped his hand. Sparks shot through his arm to his heart, then down to his cock. He longed to place her on his lap — after he found out what she needed in the bedroom.

"Are you afraid of being with two men?" Justin asked.

Her eyes widened. "Bold."

"He can be." Martin shook his head. The bastard did like to be blunt. "The floor is yours. Please, tell us what you like."

She shifted her gaze between him and Justin. "I haven't ever been with two men at once, but I would like both of you to be in control. I like submitting. I like spanking, too. I have no problem using my safe word, but I also like to be restrained, spanked, directed and to use toys. I would love to be on my knees between you, blowing both of you."

Justin rubbed the growing bulge in his jeans. "I see."

So did Martin. He rubbed the back of her hand. "What don't you want to do? Or don't like?"

"Blood." She blushed. "I don't like blood. Makes me sick to my stomach. I don't want to be denigrated and I also don't want to be foisted off to other men. If I'm going to play with you, I will get my heart involved, so if that's not what you want, then tell me now."

"Doesn't bother me," Martin said. He wasn't going to share her with anyone else besides Justin.

"I don't share, unless it's with Martin." Justin palmed her thigh. "You're safe that way."

"Thank you." She relaxed a bit. "Don't beat me and leave marks. I'd prefer you don't beat me, to be honest."

Martin bristled. Who in the fuck beat her? *Why* had they beaten her? "We won't."

The corner of Justin's right eye twitched — his tell her words pissed him off. "Who did that?"

"Did what?" Chloe asked. "Hurt me?"

"Yes. No one has the right to do that." The muscle in Justin's jaw clenched. "Ever."

"He's right. They don't, but we guarantee we won't do that to you. If you're our sub, then you're safe with us." Martin continued to caress her hand. "The collar I put on you was simply to let everyone else here know you belong to us."

"So no one else approaches you," Justin said. "So you can decide what you want."

"Thank you." She exhaled and closed her eyes. "I want to submit to you. If I could plan out this scene, I'd like to submit and drop to my knees. Kneel between you. Withdraw your cocks and switch between the two as I lick you. You thread your fingers in my hair, directing me. I can't touch myself because you're in charge. You make me wait. You stand me up, bind my hands, then strip me."

"Is that all?" Justin murmured. He kissed her shoulder again.

"No." She tipped her head, offering her neck. "There's more."

"What?" Martin moved over to the sofa and situated her between his legs. He tipped her head back and kissed her, preventing her from speaking. He didn't care. The scene had a start and he had an idea where to take it. When he broke the kiss, she whimpered.

"I want to submit to you." She slid her palm over Martin's chest.

"We need your safe word." Justin nibbled on her shoulder. "And an agreement."

"We will spank you, strip you, plant you between us," Martin said. "While one fucks you, the other uses that beautiful mouth."

She groaned and arched into Martin's touch. "Yes. Please."

"Tell us your safe word, babe." Justin eased his arm around her waist and moved his hand to her breast. "Tell us."

She quivered. "Uh..." Her head lolled and she panted. "Stop. My safe word is stop, but I don't want to use it yet."

"You have the right to use it at any time," Martin said. "We expect it."

"Yes, sirs."

Martin put space between them, then stood. "Do you want to play?"

"Yes." She didn't open her eyes. She pushed into Justin, giving him better access to her breasts.

"Beautiful." Justin squeezed her chest. "Stand up. We want to get a good look at you."

She managed to look at Martin, then complied. She wobbled to her feet and clasped her hands behind her back. "Yes, sirs."

Martin stalked around her. "I want you to talk while we play. Want you to tell me you like what we're doing or not. Understand?"

"Yes, sirs." She bowed her head. "I do."

He swatted her ass, loving the sound of the latex snap. God, she had a great ass, too. Just enough to smack and with a pleasant little jiggle. "We expect you to tell us if you're not happy. Don't hold anything back."

"Yes, sirs." She widened her stance. "May I have another?"

"Another what?" He moved her hair off the back of her neck, exposing the zipper to her dress and the sensitive flesh. "Hmm?"

"Another spanking, sir. I deserve it." She flexed her hands. "I've been a bad girl."

"How so?" He settled on the couch and patted his lap. "Come here and show me what you want?"

She didn't look at him, but scampered over to him.

Before she could do anything else, Justin stopped her. He inched up behind her and placed his hand on her shoulder. "Still."

She froze as Justin unzipped the tight dress. In seconds, the garment slipped to the floor. She stood before them in nothing but her high-heeled shoes. Her nipples tightened and she sucked in her belly. Her legs quivered.

Martin swept his gaze over her and drank in the view. Christ, she made him rock hard and difficult to fight the desire to take her right now. He wanted to kiss every inch of her, to feel the softness of her skin under his hands. Blood rushed to his cock. His skin sizzled and he patted his lap. "Come here."

She flicked her gaze to Justin, then complied. Planting her hands on the floor, she stretched across Martin's thighs and exposed her ass.

"Good girl." He trailed his fingers over her backside. "You've been a bad girl? How? Tell me?"

"I watched those people out there and wished I could be one of them. I wanted to play with them," she said. Her voice caught. "I want to be where they are."

"Do you?" He spanked her hard on the right side of her ass. "Count them."

"Yes, sir. One." She groaned. "May I have another?"

He said nothing and swatted her three more times, peppering her backside. Her skin blossomed red.

"Two, three, four," she said. "Thank you, sir. May I have another?"

Justin dropped to his knees before her and opened his pants. "Show me you want this."

She whimpered. "Sirs."

Martin spanked her three more times, ensuring her ass would be red and hot by the time he finished. As he swatted her, Justin stroked himself. She leaned forward and swallowed him to the root. The action cut off any chance she could answer Martin, but he didn't care. Martin spanked her again. Before the night concluded, he wanted her to feel them in her soul and know they wanted to be with her. This wasn't a one-night adventure. He wanted much longer than that.

She bobbed her head, pleasuring Justin while Martin spanked her.

Martin smoothed his hands over her abused butt. He'd have to massage some cream onto the tender skin before the night ended. He swatted her hip. "Stand."

She let go of Justin's dick with a pop, then wobbled to her feet. Her hair fell into her eyes and she panted.

"Do you want us to use you?" Martin asked. He angled her so she faced Justin. His cousin sat on the couch with his pants open. "Show him you want him."

She leaned over and resumed blowing him. She bobbed her head and waggled her ass. Martin marveled at her body. How could he not want to fuck her? He grabbed a condom from the cabinet, then unzipped his jeans and shoved the tight denim down his thighs. Once he sheathed himself, he grasped her hips and lined himself up with her pussy. He pushed into her in one thrust.

"Fuck," he cried out. God, she was tight. She practically held him inside her. He fit perfectly in her and never wanted to leave.

"Yes." Justin threaded his fingers into her hair and held on to her head. He guided her forward, helping to build the steady rhythm.

Martin fell right into the cadence of their actions, pushing her toward Justin, then nearly pulling out. Being with her felt right. Like this was what they were supposed to be doing, where they were supposed to be. The three of them belonged in this moment together.

He lost himself in the sheer thrill of fucking her, then leaned over her and eased his hand between her pussy lips. He caressed her clit, making her cry out around Justin's cock.

"Yes, babe. Let go and enjoy this." Martin spanked her with his free hand while continuing to pump into her and play with her clit. He wanted her to lose control just as much as she managed to scatter his thoughts.

"Come for us," Justin said. "Fuck. I love that mouth. You feel like heaven around me." He groaned and let go of her hair. He slapped at the couch cushion. When he tipped his head back, he shivered and jerked forward.

Martin knew that reaction. Justin was right at the edge of coming. He wanted to tell his cousin to let go, but the words were gone. He couldn't think straight, much less talk. All he could do was continue to fuck Chloe and focus on her. He smoothed his fingers back to her pussy lips, using her own cream to lubricate her clit, and continued to rub her. He leaned over her.

"Come for me," Martin whispered. He wasn't going to be able to hold back for much longer. The sweet scent of her, the softness of her skin, the way she whimpered when he fucked her and the thrill of being complete were too much for him to handle. He growled and rammed into her, losing his sense of rhythm. The world seemed to melt away except for her and this moment.

"Fuck," Justin shouted and pushed hard. He sagged on the couch and panted. "Fuck, I love that." He petted her hair. The groan resonating from him echoed in the room.

So did he. Martin continued to caress her clit, pushing her closer to coming apart.

She rested her head on Justin's thigh and clawed at his bunched-up pants around his knees. "I can't..." She tensed, then writhed. "I need to come."

"Come for us," Martin and Justin said in tandem.

Martin swatted her once more, then pinched her clit with his other hand.

She cried out and tensed. Whatever she said as she whimpered was lost against Justin's thigh. She trembled. "My God."

Feeling her orgasm around his cock, squeezing him and keeping him within her body was more than he could handle. He gave into the rising climax and allowed himself to tumble over the edge. He surged into her and stayed rooted in her body while the orgasm washed through him. He flattened his hand on her clit and wrapped his other arm around her waist.

"God, I love that." Justin laughed, then sighed. "Yes."

Martin loved what they'd done, too. His body relaxed, but his mind raced. He had to figure out how they could keep Chloe in their life. He'd had a taste of her and he wasn't about to lose that now.

Martin pulled out and let go, then guided her to the couch. He removed the condom and tossed the used rubber into the nearby wastebasket, then placed her on his lap and rested her head on his shoulder. Justin arranged her legs on his, holding her.

"I don't know what to think." She toyed with the wrinkles in Martin's shirt. "This has been more than I could ever expect."

"It's just the start," Justin said. "We're rather fond of you."

He hadn't wanted his cousin to be this bold, but Justin was right. They had become rather fond of her in a short period of time. Still, he wanted to wait just a little longer. Get to know her better. Sure, he knew her on paper, but paper and personality were two different things.

"You are?" Her voice came out strained, but she barely moved. "How? It's only been one time."

"Then why don't we have an encore?" Martin asked. "And a few dates?"

"Encore tonight?" she asked. "I can't even stand."

"Not tonight, sweet girl." He patted her hip. "You need to rest."

"I'm not even sure how I'm going to drive home."
She managed to sit up. "My ass is sore. I regret nothing,
but it's sore." She flattened her hand on Martin's chest,
then switched her gaze between him and Justin.

"You don't have to drive yourself home." Justin
caressed her leg. "We'll have you taken home."

"I drove." She covered her nudity. "I should go."

"Wait." Martin stilled her hands. "Talk to us. Please.
Why do you need to go?"

"I have to take care of my... I have to take care of
Madelin." She sat up, then scooted off his lap. "She can
take care of herself, but I said I'd be there for her. I
shouldn't be here having a good time when she's on her
own."

"Slow down." Martin stood, yanked his pants back
up and tucked himself behind his boxer briefs, then
gathered her in his arms. "Who is Madelin?" He hadn't
found her name in his research.

"Talk to us." Justin embraced her as well. "We're
here for you."

"It's too complicated." She wriggled, trying to get
free. "Please."

"How about you please answer us?" Martin didn't
let go. "I don't mind helping you. We'd prefer to help
you. Talk to us."

"I have to be an adult. I can't keep playing this
fantasy game right now and need to go. The real world
isn't waiting because I want something." She managed
to get free, then snatched her dress from the floor.
"Thank you for the best night of my life. I'll cherish it
always and never forget you."

Martin shook his head. She wasn't leaving them
without a backward glance again. No way. He stepped
between her and the door, stopping her.

"You're going to prevent me from leaving?" she asked and held the dress in front of her. "I need to go."

"You didn't five minutes ago." He brushed her hair from her face. "I don't know what's going on here, but we would like to see you again. Give us that chance. Please?"

She hesitated as Justin enveloped her in a robe. "Thanks." She shook her head. "I do want to see you again, but I'm not the kind of woman you want to be wrapped up with. You're powerful men and I'm a mess."

"You can't be that much of a mess." Martin rested his forehead on hers. "Give us a chance."

"I will," she said. "Just not tonight. I need to go." She ducked around him and darted out of the room.

Justin groaned. "We really have to get her to stop doing that and get her to trust us."

Martin shook his head, but he wasn't as worried as he'd thought he might be. "She will. This all happened for a reason and we're not the kind of guys to let a good thing get away."

They'd find her again and soon, she'd be theirs.

Always.

Chapter Five

Chloe hurried out of the room and out to the foyer. The robe would be fine to get her home, but she needed to have something else on in case Madelin wanted her to pick her up from her friend's. The last thing she needed was to explain to a fourteen year old what she'd been doing. She rushed to the changing room and switched back into her dress, but just barely. She groaned. Why hadn't she chosen something easier to wear? If there was a next time, she'd wear something satin and less complicated.

She finished, but kept the robe in hand as she returned to the desk. The doorman, Danny, rounded the corner. "Hello."

"You're ready to leave already?" Danny asked. "Did you not have fun?"

"I had a wonderful time." She offered over the robe. "Too much."

"Then you'll be returning?"

"I hope to." But her hope wasn't high.

"Oh?" He retrieved her purse, keys and thin coat, then pushed the robe back to her. "Honey, you need that more than we do. Consider it a gift."

She glanced down at her outfit. Everything was back in the dress where it belonged. "I don't get it."

"You're heading home for a reason. Boyfriend? Husband? Child? Or some emergency, yes?"

She swore she burned from her hairline to her toes. "Yes. A child. She's at a friend's, but I have to pick her up."

"There's no shame in that, but she won't want to see you dressed like that." He flicked his fingers. "So take it."

She wrestled back into the robe and part of her was thankful he'd offered the garment to her for a way to hide what she'd been doing.

"I admire anyone who raises kids. Anyone who works with kids. I don't have it in me. Working here is almost like herding cats, so I can't imagine doing the same with children. I have no plans as to having kids, but still." He stood in the doorway to his little office and folded his arms. "You're permitted to come back, you know. We hope your next visit will last longer and we'd love to see you again soon. I know life gets in the way, but you're welcome to return. I'm guessing you had a great time and the hunger will be there to come back."

"Thank you." She appreciated his understanding. "I just come in again? No special cards or anything?"

"You come in and I'll remember you." He smiled and waved. "Have a good night and use those sexy memories of your time here to propel you to come back sooner than later."

"Thank you." She held tight to her keys and hurried out the door to the parking garage, then to her car. Once behind the wheel, she locked the vehicle and checked her phone. Only ten-thirty. Good. She wasn't late to pick up Madelin. She cursed Melinda for not being the parent Madelin needed. Maybe this whole charade, though, was a teaching tool for them all. Madelin knew she had a refuge when things went wrong, Having the teenager around forced Chloe to work on her patience, but her sister? Who the hell knew what this was teaching anyone?

She drove back to her apartment long enough to change her clothes, switching into a pair of denim shorts and a sloppy T-shirt, plus ballet flats, then hurried across town to pick up her niece. As much as she liked Madelin, she'd much rather be back at the club with Justin and Martin. They knew how to touch her and make her scream. How to make her weak in the knees. She longed to stay with them. Let them take care of her and never leave their arms.

But that was silly.

Staying in someone's arms wasn't feasible. Everyone had to work. Had to do something to make money. She had no idea what Justin or Martin might do for a profession. They gave off an air of class, but anyone could have that. They could fake it, too.

She shook her head and pulled to a stop in front of the split-level home. Madelin sat on the front porch. The second she saw the car, she raced to the vehicle.

"What's wrong?" She waited for Madelin to shut the door. "Do you need to tell them you're leaving?"

"No." Madelin curled into herself and began to cry. "Why didn't you come sooner?"

"I said eleven." She glanced at the clock. "It's not even eleven."

"You were supposed to know."

Teens. She was still learning what to do and her niece expected clairvoyance. "Know what?" She pulled away and got them far from the house to a parking lot before she questioned Madelin more. She stopped in the shopping center lot under one of the lights. "Please, tell me what's going on? I thought you were excited to spend the night with your friends — not your mom."

Madelin kept her knees to her chest. Tears stained her cheeks. "I went there to see Mom. I thought if Mom could see I was doing okay, she'd ask me to come home."

"She didn't?" She pulled a tissue from her purse to offer to Madelin. "Honey, why wouldn't she let you come home?" The last she knew, Melinda wanted Mad to be home and was irritated she'd run away.

"She threw me out because Kindra and I kissed." Madelin buried her face in her knees and sobbed.

"Honey." She reached across the console and hugged Madelin. "I'm sorry."

"You don't like what we did, either." Madelin sobbed against her. "You're mad, too. She said everyone would hate me."

"No." She hugged Mad tighter. "There's nothing wrong with what you did. Nothing at all. You kissed, and you're a kid. You're trying to figure things out and that's not bad. It's human and I'm not upset with you at all about that. I'm not upset with you at all." But she did have a big problem.

"We tried to have Mom talk to her mom to prove things were okay."

"And?"

"Mom freaked out." Madelin continued to cry. "She said we were messing around and had to grow up. Stop being babies. Life isn't fair and you have to make decisions. Do what's right."

"You're not a baby and you're not an adult yet. You're allowed to be a kid and not to have all your choices make sense." She petted Madelin's hair. "You're becoming an adult."

Madelin still sobbed, but didn't speak.

"You're fourteen and figuring things out. It's okay to question. Does Kindra make you feel good?"

"She's my best friend."

"Did she mind you kissing her?"

"Kind of, but I don't know." Madelin shook her head. "We practiced. She's got a boyfriend and she wanted to practice kissing me to make sure when she kissed him, she wouldn't mess it up. I like practicing because then when I finally kiss a boy, I'll do it right and won't screw it up."

Oh good God. Practice. This wasn't nearly the big issue Melinda thought. "You won't screw it up, but even if you do, then it's not a big thing. Everyone has to start somewhere and most of us with a lack of experience. It's okay." She offered another tissue, she sighed. "Do you like Kindra? Like that?"

"I don't know. I don't know how I feel. She's my best friend and I like kissing her, but I don't know if I like her. I like Crowley and Sam, too. I don't know." Madelin began to cry harder. "Kindra is my friend and I like kissing her, but I don't know. Do I have to know? Right now? It's all a mess."

"Slow down." She tried to stay calm. Madelin didn't need her anger, especially since it wasn't for her. She needed understanding. "We'll get this figured out. Your mom will come around, but right now we need to cool this off."

"With Kindra?"

"No." She let go of her niece and adjusted her seatbelt. "Let's go home. You don't have to have everything figured out right now. If you did, I'd be surprised, because it's a lot to comb through. You just need time and experience to know what you want, and your mother needs to calm down. Everyone needs a few minutes to relax."

"You're really not mad?"

"Why should I be mad? You haven't done anything wrong." She drove them back to the apartment and parked in her spot outside of the building. She wasn't sure how to fix this with her family, but getting angry with anyone wasn't going to make things better. It'd screw it up even more. Right now, they needed to cool the situation off and get some rest. "Come on. Girls' night for the rest of the night."

She'd rather be with Justin and Martin, delighting in their touch, but Madelin needed her more. The dream of those men would have to wait.

Maybe forever.

"With ice cream?" Madelin asked. "We have some."

She walked with Mad to the apartment. "I know. I bought it, remember?" She laughed. "We'll have ice cream and figure out what to do...after we find something to watch."

"A rom-com?" Madelin followed her into the apartment. "Something sappy?"

"You bet." She closed the door behind them. "When do you have band practice in the morning?"

"It's Friday, so not until noon. School starts next Tuesday and we're getting ready for the first football game." Madelin left her bag by the door. "Kindra's mom will give me a ride, so you can go to work."

"I wasn't worried about it." She hugged her niece. She'd thought school started soon and she'd have to adjust her schedule. Her head hurt and she remembered why she'd chosen not to have kids. This was all too complicated. "I don't know why your mom is being this way, but she's confused. She's trying to understand this, and you both need time."

"So I can stay here a little longer?" Madelin let go and opened the freezer. She withdrew the box of ice cream.

"You can." She kicked out of her shoes. "So what happened?"

Madelin sat on the counter. "I went to Kindra's so we could watch a movie and a couple times we've practiced kissing. I like kissing her because she smells good and she makes me feel good. She feels the same way, but she thinks she should be dating Corey. I don't know who I want to date, but I like kissing her and I like watching movies with Sam. Besides, I'm a kid. Tomorrow, I might decide I like Corey. I doubt it, because he likes Kindra and he's too short for me."

"Then it's okay." She grabbed two spoons from the drawer. "When I was your age, I had a friend that I experimented with, too. It's okay. You figure out what you like and how you want to proceed. You're too young to be dating anyone, but if you kissed Kindra, then it's okay. You don't have to decide right now what you want."

"Thanks." Madelin dug into the rocky road ice cream. "I asked Mom to come over to Kindra's so we could talk and I could tell her that. I don't know what I want, but I want her to love me. All she heard was who I kissed and flipped out."

"This isn't a simple issue, so give her time. Right now, we have ice cream to eat." She dug her spoon into the creamy mess.

"How was your date?"

She froze, spoon halfway to her mouth. "How did you know I went on a date?"

"You got dressed up. That dress was fantastic, by the way." Madelin ate a bite of the ice cream. "I saw it on your bed. I wanted to try it on, but I didn't."

"Oh." She hadn't realized she'd seen it. "I..." She didn't want her niece wearing a latex dress, much less finding the one she'd worn. She'd have to hide certain pieces of her wardrobe a little better.

"So was it a good date? Is he cute?"

"He is. They are." *Shit.* She hadn't wanted to tell Madelin about both men, especially since she wasn't exactly dating them both.

"Two? You went on two dates?"

"Kind of, but not really." She wasn't about to tell Madelin about the club. "They're friends and we all went out."

"Oh nice. Like when Kindra, Sam, Crowley, Corey and I went to the movies."

"Yes." Close enough. "They're my friends and we had a good time."

"In that dress, you should've." Madelin ate more of the ice cream. "I pay a lot more attention than people think. I know Mom's been cheating on David. Has been for the last three years. The guy's name is Earl. He comes over every weekend while David's at work. She tells David she's just tired and he buys it."

She stared at Madelin. "She's so bold as to do it in front of you?"

"She sends me to camp and that's part of the reason I ran away. I'm tired of watching her make him a fool." Madelin abandoned her spoon in the sink. "She doesn't love David, which I guess is okay. People don't have to be together forever, but she's mad at me for who I kissed and she's doing that. David has an idea what's going on, but he's still in love with her. She's treating him like shit and there's nothing anyone can do."

Madelin's insights were much more spot-on than anyone probably realized. She paid a lot more attention than she was given credit for doing.

"It's ridiculous. I don't know what she thinks she's doing, but it's not nice. She's hurting David, making a fool of Earl and she pushes me away so she can do what she wants. I get it. I'm not David's or Earl's and I'm in the way." Madelin inched away from Chloe. "She pushes me out. I don't know if she's really upset about Kindra."

"She's wrapped up in her own drama and taking it out on you." She grabbed Madelin in a hug. The kid was dealing with something heavier than most kids should ever have to, and with quite a bit of maturity. She sighed and held on to Madelin. Why did people do this to each other? Treat each other so terribly?

"She wants me out of the house so she can lie to David. She even told me to live with Dad." Madelin sobbed. "Dad doesn't want me, either. He's busy with whichever girlfriend he's got right now."

She wasn't sure what she was going to do, but she had to sort this all out. Madelin deserved better. "Okay. I'll talk to your mother, but you hang out. I'm not making you leave."

"Why do you want me? Why aren't you trying to get rid of me, too? You should be living. You're the one who should be having fun." Madelin sobbed. "You don't need me."

"Are you kidding?" She guided her niece to the couch and sat beside her. "You're a lot of fun. Who else will eat ice cream with me? Who else is going to peek at my clothes and give me fashion advice?"

"You do need to up your liner game."

She should've expected that. "Then you'll have to give me some tutorials."

"Before your next date?"

She nodded and laughed. Of course her niece would have this insight. "You're going to ensure I go on another date?"

"Yeah. I don't know what these guys look like, but someone should be happy." Madelin finally smiled. "You gotta love who you love and maybe these guys are the ones you should love."

"When did you get to be so smart?" She hugged her niece. "You're too smart for your own good."

"I try." Madelin dried her face. "I should go to bed. You've got work and I've got practice."

"I'm going to be at the first football game. Right out front, shouting and cheering for my favorite band kid." She stood. "I'm proud of you."

"Thanks, Aunt Chloe." Madelin hesitated, then ducked into the guest bedroom.

Chloe sank back onto the couch and covered her face in her hands. She'd waded into something deeper than she'd ever expected. Between the situation with Martin and Justin that she wasn't even sure was a thing, then her sister and Madelin...why did life have to be so complicated?

Her wants weren't her own any longer. She had to think about her niece. So much for having a love life. The guys could wait.

Of course.

Love could wait, too. She had memories of her night with them. Her body ached in places she'd long ignored. Her ass hurt from the spanking and she'd done some deliciously naughty things, but they'd have to wait. She had a duty to her family.

She didn't need love, did she?

Chapter Six

Justin paced the length of his office. He hated pacing, but he wasn't sure what else to do. He didn't like waiting for anything, much less something he desired.

His irritation grew with each step. How could she just walk away? Just give up on the chance to have everything she wanted, if she'd have stuck around? If she'd have asked questions. If she'd have paid attention.

This wasn't the first time he'd been denied, but it rankled him more than anything. Molly hadn't stuck around, either. Granted, he'd decided to walk away from her first, but that didn't mean much. When he chose someone, he was the one to break it off — not her. Chauvinistic, he knew, but he'd grown so accustomed to getting what he wanted that when he didn't, his anger got the best of him.

He really needed to cool off, but the more he moved, the more he wanted to demand his desires.

"Stop." Martin stepped into Justin's path. "Relax."

He glared at his brother. "She just left us. Three days ago, she boogied right out. No word, nothing. Why? How?" His irritation moved past fury to anger. Why was he so pissed? Because he wasn't getting what he wanted.

"I know what happened. I was there."

"You're not upset?" He flexed his hands. His cousin could be so calm. So collected. Not him. He was the one who flew off the handle. He shouted. Gesticulated. He'd never understand how Martin could be so cool under pressure.

At the same time, Justin wasn't used to being blown off. Wasn't used to being ignored. He hated that both had happened, yet he kind of liked it. She was making him work for what he wanted.

Damn her.

"I'm not." Martin shrugged and stayed in Justin's path. "And you shouldn't be, either."

"Why?" He folded his arms and widened his stance. "Tell me."

"Because you're going full fury without reason," Martin said. "I did some sleuthing and found out a few things. She ran out, but it wasn't for nothing. She's been trying to help raise her niece. She left so she could handle that situation—much like you and I when we've had to go to job sites and sort out problems. We go, handle it and move on to the next problem. Yes?"

He had to agree, but he refused to verbalize it. He needed a few minutes to process what he'd been told. *A niece. Raising a kid.* Well, hell. Everything did square more easily now. He'd never had kids or even dated someone with kids, but if she had to go, then she did.

Still, his fuse was lit. "Why? Why is she doing that? Doesn't her sister or whatever have custody?"

"You're not being kind," Martin snapped. "I don't know why she's doing it and this is her story to tell, but we'll have to get it from her. We'll have to be patient — meaning you'll have to cool it before you talk to her. If you go off, then you'll screw this up for us."

Martin was right. Justin sighed and tried to turn down his frustration. "Is she too busy for us?"

"It seems," Martin said and paused. "Are you changing your mind?"

"About her?"

"About her." Martin remained in his path. "Are you?"

"No." Not at all. Her situation was a lot to take in, but he wasn't deterred.

"Then what?"

His fury finally melted and he accepted a bit of defeat. "God."

"What?"

"I'm not used to being set aside," he growled. This wasn't how the story was supposed to go. She should've accepted their invitation to come home, to play and then to become their toy for the weekend before realizing they were meant to be together and staying with them. They'd whisk her from her situation and save her.

Except that wasn't how the scene played out. She'd been their girl, but life had pushed into their little world.

"You don't like it, do you?" Martin asked.

"No."

"Then you're in for a world of hurt." Martin walked away to his desk and turned his back on Justin. "Things won't always go our way."

"But it doesn't usually happen to me. I don't have to worry about things not going my way." Not in designs, not in building, not in life. When he wanted something, he got it. Most of the time, he not only got it, but he was given even more.

"Aren't you a demanding prick?" Martin asked. He leaned on his desk. "It's been too soft for us. We haven't had to work this hard, you're right, for anything, in a long time. It's time we do that, isn't it?"

He glared at Martin. Once again, Martin didn't have to be right or so calm. The bastard. It wasn't fair. "Maybe I am."

"Which is your problem." Martin crossed his ankles and stared at him. "A woman worth having is worth waiting for and she's both."

He hated when Martin was correct…again. "Fine."

"We've been handed so much and it's time we have to put in some effort," Martin said. "When I met Cindy, she didn't just throw herself at me. She made me work for her affections. She made me think about what I wanted and do something about it. She gave me grief, but she was worth it. I believe Chloe is the same, but unlike Cindy, she's worth both of us putting in the work. There is a potential she could be the one for the both of us, if we give her a chance. I know we can."

"I know." He sighed, deflated and convinced he needed to change his mindset. "True."

"I get it, though. I want her. I want her in our bed, our lives and our home, but it's not possible right now. I don't doubt she's meant to be ours, but it'll take time. When things finally all come around, it'll be sweeter."

He nodded. "Like a prize." A sexy, curvy, soft prize.

"Or like a treasure. She's more of a gem, than just a piece of glass or gold-covered plastic."

He had to concede on that point. He'd been looking at the whole situation from the wrong perspective. He and Martin didn't have to work for much. Due to their inheritances and investments, they had enough to not only live comfortably, but with plenty of time to do as they pleased. They'd expected so much, but now they'd have to be patient in order to get their treasure.

He could be patient.

He just wanted her. Even after only three days, he missed holding her, listening to her heartbeat, watching her get frazzled... He wanted to get to know her. To know what made her tick. What made her sad. Did she like flowers? Or was she more of a plant them and look, not pick kind of girl? He wanted to find out.

The sex was already off the charts. She'd become an addiction and he wanted more.

Unfortunately, he'd have to wait.

"I came into your office to speak to you about the Lunney contracts. They're ready for us to sign and we've got an appointment in an hour with the Reid Firm to go over them," Martin said. "Since the Lunney account is so big, I'd like to make sure this is done properly."

"I know." He had to pull himself together and fast. Not a problem. He might not be good at holding his emotions in check, but he could handle switching gears to prepare for this meeting.

"Besides, I have a huge secret for you when we get there." Martin left the room, walking away before Justin could ask questions.

Justin shook his head and gathered his coat. He tucked his phone and wallet into his pockets, then headed to the lobby. His office was his safe place. No one bothered him at the office, but still. He could take his shoes off, loosen his tie and create in his space. Could draw and stay up all hours of the night, then turn around and give his cousin his drawings for the different jobs. While Martin presented the art and worked on the deals, he stayed creative. Martin knew what permits to get and how to find the right contractors for each job.

He hurried out to the car and settled in the backseat. Martin patted his pocket.

"Forgot something?" Justin asked.

"No, I had to ensure I had my phone." Martin stretched his legs. "I hate leaving the office, unless we're heading home. I hate going into the wild."

"You're so old." He laughed, despite only being two years younger than Martin. He loved to tease his cousin about their ages. "You'd forget your head if it wasn't attached."

"I might." Martin drummed his fingers. "It's funny. We've waited so long for someone like Chloe, and now she's around, we can't wait to spend more time with her. It's like the whole cosmos wants us to work for this."

"I'm sure they do." Whatever or whoever was in charge...he didn't care. As long as eventually, he and Martin came into Chloe's orbit more often, then he'd be fine. "I shouldn't trust you so much with these contracts. I let you handle the cash and the permits while I don't do dick about them."

"Maybe not, but it's fine. You're not a numbers person."

"No." He knew colors. Trying to do spreadsheets made his head hurt.

"We're here." Martin slapped Justin's arm. "Let's go."

When the car stopped, Martin left the vehicle first. He rushed away, up to the building. Justin barely kept up. He quickened his pace to follow his cousin into the firm's plush building. He loved visiting the lawyer's office because of the thick carpets and dark wood. The place was so elegant and fantastic, but full of class and elegance. He'd tried to pattern his own office after their classy look.

He walked into the foyer and up to the elevator. "You sprinted from me. Is the surprise coming first?"

"Contracts, then surprises." Martin fiddled with his phone, then pointed to the doors as they opened. "Magic."

He rolled his eyes. Nothing about what they were doing was magic. It was a contract signing. He sighed and followed Martin into the offices. He'd been to the Reid Firm a hundred times. They were the only lawyers he and Martin trusted to do any legal work for them. He strode across the room, past the bank of cubicles, then back to the private offices.

"Where's Gert?" Justin asked. "I thought she was still here."

"She got canned when she stole money." Martin stopped at the desk. The woman smiled. "We're here for the twelve-fifteen with Nathan Reid."

"Ah, yes." The woman tapped a button on her desk. "He's expecting you."

"Thanks." Martin led the way and walked from Justin.

Justin fought the urge to roll his eyes again and glanced over his shoulder. Something pulled him toward the outer area, but he made his way into the office.

Nathan sat on his desk with his hands folded. "Gentlemen." He left the desk and offered his hand. "Good to see you."

"Thanks." Justin shook hands with Nathan. "Thanks for writing this up."

"I simply took the information you gave me and plunked it in where it needed to go." Nathan winked. "I'm having drinks brought in. This calls for a celebration. This is, what, your fiftieth contract like this?"

"Fifty-third," Martin said. "But I'm all for a good celebration."

"First, let's sign these. I've gone over everything and it's all in order. I sent them to Martin to peruse before you showed up today. Any questions?" Nathan asked, and set out three rocks glasses for their drinks.

He trusted his cousin to make the proper decision. "If Marty says they're fine, then I'm good."

"I went over them three times today." Martin accepted a pen and signed where stipulated. He offered the pen and pages to Justin. "Your turn."

"You've got it." He signed where indicated and read quickly through the documents. He and his cousin were going to make quite a fortune on this deal. He remembered the renderings he'd done for the initial designs and looked forward to overseeing the project from afar. The true overseeing was Martin's job.

"Fantastic." Nathan signaled to the woman at the doorway. "Have these filed."

The woman Justin recognized as the secretary from the outer office nodded and took the documents. She returned a moment later with folios for Martin and Justin, then left again.

"Your copies." Nathan offered them each a rocks glass filled with two fingers of bourbon. "A toast."

He accepted his glass and held it up. "I love a good toast."

"To contracts, new jobs and success," Nathan said.

"And to new beginnings," Martin added. "To us."

"To all of us," Nathan said. "Enjoy."

Justin would. He loved an aged bourbon more than he should. He rolled the drink around in the glass, stirring up the aromatics and breathing it in. Intoxicating. Almost as much as Chloe. He slowly took a sip, letting the taste of the liquor spread across his tongue. As the bourbon slid down his throat, his cells burned, but he didn't care. The bite was worth it.

"I can't wait to tell you about the woman we've met," Martin said. "She's beyond compare."

"Oh?" Nathan sipped the drink. "It's good when you finally meet the one. Think she is?"

Justin shifted in his seat. The change of tone bothered him. "She might be." He had the feeling she was, but they had to find a way to have more time with her.

"So? Who is she?" Nathan asked and pulled a thick chair over to sit with them. "Where'd you meet her?"

"First ran into her at Tracks, then at Sixxes." Justin sipped his own drink. The tart liquid burned on the way down all over again.

"Oh?" Nathan asked. He and Martin grinned, but Martin didn't speak.

"What?" Justin held on to his glass. "You two know something. Tell me." He loved that Martin was a little older and more sophisticated, but could sometimes act like an older brother — smarter, savvier and more knowing.

"Remember how I mentioned there was a surprise?" Martin asked. "She's here."

He needed a moment. "What?" It wasn't possible. Chloe? There? Was she an employee? He hadn't asked her about her work and Martin hadn't offered that detail. If she walked in right now, he'd be shocked, but thrilled.

Nathan downed more of his drink. "She's a wonderful girl. Darinda has nothing but nice things to say about her." He stood. "I'll give you a moment. Don't jack up my office. This isn't my personal office, but still. I don't want the cleaning staff to have to clean up a disaster."

"Ass," Justin muttered. He shifted again in his seat as the door opened. Martin and Nathan talked about Chloe like she was there, but he wouldn't believe them until she walked in.

"You asked for me, sir?" Chloe stepped into the office. "Oh. I'm sorry. I didn't mean to interrupt."

"You're not." Nathan left his glass on the desk. "I'll be right back." He left without a second glance, closing the door behind him.

Justin hopped up from his chair. "Chloe?" She was real and very much right there. He fought the urge to scramble from his seat and snatch her in a hug. He needed to feel her in his arms again.

She froze and her eyes widened. "Martin? Justin? I…"

Martin stood slowly, then abandoned his glass next to Nathan's before holding his hand out to her. "Hi, babe."

"I…" She didn't move. "You're here."

"We are." Justin inched up to his cousin. "Good to see you."

"You're lawyers?" she asked, her voice hardly above a squeak.

"No." Justin finished the bourbon. "We're in the building industry." He needed to hold her. He crossed the room to her and enveloped her in his embrace. She smelled wonderful, felt like heaven and something within him righted. God, he'd missed her.

She whimpered and embraced him back. "Hi."

"Hi." He rested his forehead on hers. "We've missed you."

Martin moved in and embraced her from behind. "We have."

"I haven't been lost." She turned in Justin's arms and faced Martin. "I've been here."

"But we didn't have a way to contact you." Justin moved her hair from her shoulder and kissed her neck.

"I should've given you my number." She wriggled in their grasp, then scooted out from between them. "I've been overwhelmed."

"I know," Martin said. "You've got a lot going on."

"Let us take care of you and take you out." Justin kissed her shoulder again. "Just get you away for an hour or two." He needed more time with her. Even a few minutes was a good start.

"A nice dinner. Dancing." Martin sighed and cupped her jaw. "You've made an impression on us."

"Have dinner with us tonight," Justin said. "Give us that chance."

"I have complications." She held up both hands. "Trust me. I'd love to go out, but I have complications at home and I can't."

"You keep evading us," Justin said. "If we were lesser men, we'd be put off."

"You're not?" she asked.

"Nope." Martin reached for her and grasped her hand. "We can work with complications. Can work with the fact you've got to be here again tomorrow morning. Just give us the chance."

"We'll make it worth your while," Justin said. "Besides, you feel this crackle, too. You feel the spark. Let's find a way to make it grow. You just have to give us the chance. Can you do that?"

She shifted her gaze between them and didn't speak for a long moment. Her pause stole Justin's breath. God. Would she accept? She might not be so thrilled once she found out he and Martin had kept tabs on her. Then again, she might be happy to have someone protecting her.

She exhaled and stared at them. "I might be crazy for accepting, but I'd love to go to dinner with you."

Chapter Seven

Chloe held her breath and waited for Martin and Justin to rescind the offer. They were here, at her work, for a logical reason. Seeing them again made her day. It made her year. She'd longed for their touch since the moment she walked away. The memory of the way they touched her, the feel of their bodies against hers and the way each of them tasted was all cemented in her mind. She'd tried in vain to ignore the hunger for them within her.

She could be foolish for going along with their demand, but she wanted to be with them again.

Justin embraced her a second time and swept her off her feet. "My God, yes." He rested his forehead on hers again and nuzzled her nose with his own. "We've worried about you."

"There's nothing to worry about." She wasn't anyone special.

"We'll pick you up after work and have dinner." Justin swayed with her. "It'll be magical."

"I can't. I have to be at a meeting." She didn't want to tell them the sticky mess with her niece. "Sorry."

"We're not taking no for an answer." Martin patted the chair. "Talk to us."

"I barely know you." She tensed in Justin's embrace. "What if you're terrible to me? What if I'm not right for you?" The sex was good—no, great—but sex wasn't everything.

"That's why we go out." Martin patted the chair again. "Come sit and tell us what's going on."

Why did she feel so comfortable with Justin and Martin? She allowed Justin to walk her to the chair. She sat between them and folded her hands on her lap. "You want the truth?"

"It'd be a good start." Justin held out his hand. "We're here."

"You don't know me," she said. "You don't realize what's involved here."

"That's why we want you to tell us." Martin scooted closer. "We've arranged for use of this office for as long as it takes."

Justin flicked his gaze to Martin for a moment, then his brow crinkled before he sighed and returned his attention to Chloe. "Talk to us, babe."

She needed a moment to center and settle. *Crap.* Talking about herself wasn't her idea of fun. "Couldn't we just fuck instead? Blow off some steam?"

"That was the idea after dinner." Martin's eyes flashed. "But after some explanation."

She didn't owe them anything, but they weren't going to do what she wanted until she did as they demanded. She crossed her legs and folded her hands on her lap. "What do you want to know?" She might as well tell them everything.

"Why you ran out would be a good place to start," Justin said. "At least some reason why."

She could do that, even if it cost her the chance at the relationship. "My family is complicated. My father had a daughter with another woman before he married my mother and once my mother found out, she and my father divorced. He had children after the split, too, so I have family I don't even know about. The older sister I know of, Melinda, and I became close when I was in high school because she decided to meet me. We didn't feel so alone."

"Makes sense." Martin picked up a glass and drank the contents.

"The problem is, my parents are both gone. Dad died of heart failure when I was nineteen and Mom was run over by a bus. Melinda and I were left with nothing but each other. I don't know my other siblings and haven't tried to meet them. But as time went on, Melinda and I weren't as close. We're still in contact, but she has one way of raising her daughter and it's not working for her right now. Her daughter, Madelin, ran away to my apartment and she's been living with me for a couple weeks. Madelin is finally starting to open up and relax. She's a complicated kid and I won't push her, but it makes having a life hard."

"I know," Martin said. "You're handling it well."

"You know?" She stared at him. "How did you know?"

Martin held tight to the glass. "By your story. It seems like you understand what's going on and have a handle on it."

"Yeah." Something didn't sound true, but she kept going. "Madelin stays with me and she's happy. Her being there makes life complicated and I don't exactly want to explain to her why I'm wearing latex dresses or going out all hours of the night. Don't really want to explain to her why I've got two men pursuing me or that I like it. Don't really want her knowing I play or explaining why my ass hurts the next day. She's fourteen and doesn't need this much information."

Justin scooted forward in his seat. "Wait, you like it? You want us to pursue you?"

She'd been a little too honest. But what did it matter? "Yes. I like both of you and I don't know anything about you. I like being around you and the way you make me feel like I'm important. But that's not sustainable. We need to get to know each other and the more you're around me, the more you may realize you don't like me."

"I doubt that." Justin glanced at Martin, then turned back to her. "You're special to us. It takes a lot to get our attention on the dance floor, but you did. You turned our head, so to speak. I'm glad you did. You gave me a reason to want to find you. I want to feel that spark again and when I'm around you, I do."

"Likewise," Martin said. "You made an impression."

She nodded. "But I have commitments. I have a life I need to handle first."

"Handle it, but let us take you out, too. We'll help you balance it all," Justin said. "If you'll give us the chance."

She didn't want to say no. She could use all the help she could get, and maybe having a steady man — or men — in her life might boost Madelin's confidence, too. "I need to pick her up after band practice. The meeting is an informal one with Melinda. I'm hoping we can form a plan for Mad, but once I understand how

Melinda feels, then maybe something can be hashed out with Madelin, so she feels safe. She should be included, no matter what."

"She should." Martin pulled his phone from his pocket. "I'll be right back." Within seconds, he disappeared through the main door.

She bowed her head. "I upset him, didn't I? Too much honesty?"

"Nope." Justin scooted his chair right beside hers. "Knowing him, he's making reservations for tonight."

"I can't seem to get a line on him. He's distant." She turned in her seat to face Justin. "My life is complicated."

"That's okay."

"How? I gave you a sob story and it looks like I'm trying to get something from you for nothing when I'm not. But this is a big mess and you should leave. Walk away from me right now."

"Nope." Justin stood. He held both hands out to her and smiled. "Come here. I don't believe you're trying to use me or anyone else."

She wanted to hesitate, but she did as she was told and allowed him to enfold her in his arms. He swayed with her, adding a bit of calm to the situation. When he smiled at her, she melted. The resolve within her to be strong and put him off completely fell apart. The sparks increased and she wanted to stay wrapped up with him.

"You're more than you know," he whispered. He rubbed her back. "Way more."

"I am?" She didn't feel that special. She stared into his eyes and the tingles in her belly increased. She'd forgotten how sexy he was and how intoxicating his blue eyes could be. She admired the faint dusting of hairs on his chin and the sculpted build of his body. He smelled like expensive cologne and sex.

"What are you thinking?" he asked. "You're a million miles away."

"I'm right here with you." She kept swaying. "Very much so."

"Yeah?" He kissed her. The move was slow, deliberate. He kept the connection soft and increased her craving. She grasped the front of his jacket and held on.

The scant hairs on his chin scraped along her jaw and the tingles increased as they surged through her body. No, this was more like full electricity. He still tasted good and she wanted more.

He slid his hand along her back, then to her ribs and around to her breast. He brushed her nipple.

The electricity intensified and she groaned. She shouldn't be kissing Justin when her boss could walk back into his office at any time. They could get caught. She could be fired.

Yet, she couldn't stop herself.

She writhed against him and wished he'd rip her clothes off. "Justin."

He kissed along her jaw to her throat. "Yeah?" He toyed with her nipple.

More electricity shot through her. She could get into so much trouble, but that thought made the act so much hotter.

With his free hand, Justin hiked up her skirt. He continued to pinch and toy with her nipple with his other hand. He bared her backside and walked her back to the desk.

The chill spread across her ass. She backed into the desk with a grunt. Her thoughts scrambled. She parted her legs. Heat surged through her body and settled in her pussy. She craved being bent over the desk and fucked right there where she could be caught.

Right now.

She whimpered into the kiss.

"Like it?" Justin spanked her. "Like the scandal?"

She nodded, unable to say more. She panted as he pushed her panties aside and speared one finger into her pussy. He smeared her juices across her cunt lips. She whimpered again. He knew just where to touch her.

"What do you want?" he murmured and resumed kissing her jaw. He worked his fingers inside her. "Tell me."

"Fuck me," she managed. She needed him to take control and fuck her.

"I see you're still wearing our collar." He squeezed her nipple, then switched to the other breast. "You're gorgeous wearing it. Gorgeous either way."

She'd never considered herself that way, but she did love wearing the collar. It reminded her of their time together.

"I want you right here." Justin yanked her panties down, then nudged her back to the desk. "Up."

She did as he'd asked and parted her legs again. She braced her hands on the edge as Justin opened his zipper, then withdrew his cock. He opened a box on the desk. She barely registered that he'd plucked a condom from the wooden container. In seconds, he sheathed himself. Her mouth watered. She wanted to drop to her knees and blow him right now, but she didn't have a chance. He settled between her legs and grasped her hips. He thrust into her in one smooth gesture. He filled her to the hilt, stealing her breath.

She met his gaze. "Sir."

"Just like that." He held on to her hips and rocked his own as he pushed into her before nearly pulling out. He built into a steady rhythm in seconds. She whimpered.

Nothing else mattered. Her boss could walk in right now and she wouldn't care. She wrapped her legs around Justin's waist. The only thing that would make this better would be to have Martin join them. Call her needy, but she wanted them both.

Justin growled. "You feel so good. So fucking tight. Like you're made for me." He increased his pace, mashing her into the desk.

Heat engulfed her. She wanted to rip her clothes off. She tipped her head back and rode the waves of desire within her body.

He slipped one hand between their bodies and rubbed her clit. The combination of being fucked and having her sensitive clit touched turned her insides out. She tensed. "Justin."

"Don't you dare come yet." He pinched the tight bundle of nerves, then surged into her. He grunted as he slowed his movements. His cock throbbed as he filled her with his seed. Part of her wished he didn't have the condom on, but the rest of her appreciated him being safe. She trembled, not able to come. She needed a few more thrusts and more attention.

Justin withdrew. "Stay right there. Don't you dare move."

She didn't even try. She stared at him as he removed the spent condom and tossed it in the trash, then put himself back behind his zipper and righted his clothes. Did he want her to get fired? Nathan would surely fire her for being so brazen on his desk.

The door opened and she nearly screamed. Instead of Nathan walking into the office, Martin ventured into the room.

"What do we have here?" Martin stalked across the carpet to the desk. "I leave for a moment and you're getting busy together?"

"I want you, too." She sounded so wanton, but she didn't care. She needed to come and craved his cock inside her, too. She braced her hands on the desk. "Want both of you."

"Soon." Martin's eyes blazed. "Seeing you fucking my cousin was the hottest thing I've ever witnessed."

"Was it?" She wished she were nude. The flames engulfing her from within were almost too much to handle.

"Yes." Martin opened the same box and retrieved a condom. He tore the packaging, then stepped up to her. "You know what to do."

She leaned forward and unzipped his trousers. She met his gaze as she withdrew his dick from behind his boxer briefs. Holding him pleased her. She stroked him, getting him even harder.

"Good girl." He offered her the condom and nodded.

She accepted the rubber, then sheathed him. He rewarded her with a kiss. Unlike Justin's, which was soft and tender, Martin's was commanding and sinful. She had no chance to think. Just ride the wave of pleasure. She held on to his shoulders as he pushed into her pussy. The sheer power overwhelmed her. She wrapped her legs around Martin much like she'd done with Justin.

"God-fucking-hell-yes, that's hot," Justin said. He whipped his phone out. "Don't want to forget this. Christ."

She didn't mind being photographed. She focused on Martin and tipped her head back, then lost herself in the act of making love with Martin.

He pushed into the hilt, then pulled most of the way. Where Justin had girth, Martin had more length. He touched different parts within her. The tip of his dick rubbed across her G-spot, adding to her pleasure. She cried out.

"Martin." She clawed at his shoulders. The orgasm had been right there below the surface with Justin, now being fucked by Martin brought it right back to the forefront. She cried out again and instead of holding the climax back, she rode it along with Martin. The thrill of being used this way, having the power to control the situation and being watched all played into her desires. Into her needs. She whimpered as Martin increased his pace. Rational thought left her mind and she simply enjoyed what was happening.

Martin slammed into her. "Fuck, yes. Tell me you like this. So fucking hot."

She panted as she slipped right over the edge. "Martin." She tumbled into the orgasm. She swore she floated. The rest of the world, even Justin, seemed to melt away.

Martin growled as he pushed to the hilt into her and held her tight to his body. He seemed to vibrate as he came. He curled over her, not letting go.

She kept her arms and legs around him as she panted. Her head swam. Dear God. She'd thought being at the club was hot and it was, but this was just as sexy. She managed to open her eyes.

"Damn, babe." Justin joined them and petted her hair. "You know how to make us crazy."

"Do I?" she managed.

Martin pulled out and Justin helped her stretch back out, putting her feet on the floor. Justin kept his arm around her as she regained her bearings. Martin removed the rubber and tossed it, then straightened his clothes as he put his dick back in his pants.

"Now, how about the dinner date tonight?" Justin asked. He smoothed her skirt into place. "Please?"

She doubted he said please very often. She'd have to figure something out for that night, but she did want to have dinner with them. "I need to check my calendar."

"Oh?" Martin quirked his brow and laughed. "For other boyfriends?"

"To see if Mad has a home game or not. If it's away, then I've got more time. If it's home, then I'd like to attend the game and support her." She stood on wobbly legs and managed to right her disheveled clothes. "Is that okay?"

"It's fine." Justin kissed her tenderly. "Babe, we want you to be happy. You do what you need, but don't keep us waiting long."

Martin slipped his arm around her. "We've got you. Whatever you need, we've got you."

She liked knowing they'd take care of her, but something niggled at the back of her mind. "How...how did we not get interrupted? My boss should've come back and should be firing me right now. You have to know something about it. What did you do?"

Martin half-smiled and Justin bowed his head. Martin leveled his gaze at her. "We might have orchestrated this time alone with you. We did have to sign contracts, but we might have known about your working here."

"What?" She backed away from them. "Did you check up on me?"

Justin snapped his attention to her. "Is that bad?"

"Yes." Her skin prickled. She didn't like being watched, even if they had a good reason. They didn't have the right to do that to her. She backed away from them. "How much else have you orchestrated?"

Martin shook his head. "We cared."

"You had no right." She balled her hands. "Don't you dare call me or find me. I can't do this right now. I refuse to have my life orchestrated by anyone." She turned on her heel and walked out of the office. She'd done yet another of the hottest things in her life, but she'd leave on principle.

No one had the right to run her life. That was her job and she'd be damned if she'd let them, no matter how much money and influence they had.

Not a chance.

Chapter Eight

Martin growled, but not at her. At himself. *Jesus H. Christ.* How could he have been so foolish? He'd thought he was so smart. He'd checked up on her. He knew her schedule and where she hung out. He knew what she liked...but he hadn't gotten to know her. Hadn't romanced her. Just typical Martin and Justin, pushing and orchestrating their way through what they wanted.

Not smart.

He scrubbed both hands over his face. "We blew it again."

"We did." Justin shook his head. "We get so excited about what we want and how we're going to get it, but we don't pay attention to the collateral damage."

"Not when it comes to relationships."

The door opened a moment later and Nathan strode in. "What happened?"

"We screwed up." Martin folded his arms. "We nearly had what we wanted and we pushed too hard."

"Pushed her away?" Nathan asked.

"More or less," Justin replied. "Wasn't smart."

"You're too eager." Nathan nodded and sat on the edge of the desk. "I'll assume you first made good use of the room."

Justin tucked something into the pocket of his suit jacket. "You assume correctly."

"Then the time alone wasn't in vain." Nathan chuckled. "I get it though. When we chased Darinda, we went balls to the wall. Just headlong into what we wanted and didn't think about how she'd handle it. What it would do to her. Why should we? We're high-powered lawyers and we get what we want."

"Except there's always a question to ask." Martin wandered over to the bank of windows. "We forgot about the human element."

"You thought about it, but you got excited and assumed you knew what she wanted when you didn't. We did the same thing. We offered her a penthouse, money, clothes, whatever she wanted, but forgot to factor in love. We said, you can be our arm candy and we'll make sure you get whatever you desire. She didn't want the money, jewelry or the clothes. She wanted us. Wanted our attention in the bedroom. In the playroom."

"Oh?" Justin asked.

"You don't think you found out about her going to Sixxes by accident?" Nathan asked. "Darinda's a good spy when needed, and she helped figure out that's what Chloe wanted. She helped set the whole thing up. When I knew she'd go there, I sent word to Martin to be at the club, too."

Martin didn't have to turn around to feel the heat of his cousin's glare at his back. "It's true. Another orchestration."

"It was, but…I don't know. We can't complain. We all got what we wanted out of it," Justin said. "Just wish we'd been more forthcoming with her."

"Can I say one thing?" Nathan asked. "Coming from a friend?"

Martin glanced over his shoulder. The city beneath him was mesmerizing. All the little people coming and going. All the lives that went on without bothering anyone else. People living their every day and falling in love, falling out of love, just existing. His problem didn't mean shit in the grand scheme of things. He and Justin were two more people. Two more dots. Chloe was a dot, too.

An adorable, sweet, sensual dot that he wanted to hold on to forever.

"Are you listening to me?" Nathan asked. "Martin?"

"I doubt it," Justin said. He thumped Martin on the arm. "Hey. He's saying something important and you're ignoring him."

"Not ignoring." He turned his back on the windows. "More like thinking. We're all convinced we're so important. We've got money rolling out our ears, we wield power and people listen to us, but in the grand scheme of things, we're just another cog."

"You're right," Nathan said. "Absolutely."

"Depressing, too." Justin frowned. "Christ."

"A little." He sighed and gave Nathan his full attention. "You were saying? It's something important?"

"It was." Nathan exhaled and folded his arms. "You can chase her all day long and give her everything, but if you're all about running her life, then run the other way. She's like Darinda in that she doesn't need you to do that. She's capable. Has been since long before you showed up. What she needs is for you to say you're on her side. You'll be there for her. Listen to her. You'll take her somewhere nice, then stay all afternoon on the couch. You'll paddle her ass, if that's what she wants, then hold her while she cries. You'll both be that rock for her. She's not a business to acquire or a job to fulfill. She's a person. She's a wonderful, good worker and she seems to care about you. Don't push her away because you're busy working on what she's doing or controlling her life. Focus on making her feel like she's the only woman you can see. She's the only one who matters."

He nodded. "We can do that."

"Stop following her or delving into her past — she'll tell you about that when she's ready," Nathan said. "Act like you're the same two guys I met years ago who were clawing and hustling to get their business off the ground and genuinely cared. That's who she needs."

"Martin's right. We can do that and more." Justin shoved his hands into his pockets. "She's the one we want."

"Give her some time, for the most part," Nathan said. He slipped a piece of paper into Martin's hand. "By the way, she doesn't seem to want to see you, so I'd suggest giving her space, too. If you head out the way you came in, you won't run into each other."

"Thanks." He pocketed the paper and bowed his head. "Thanks for the advice. We're eager, but we're willing to learn."

"I know you are. When you finally find that one, it's easy to get ahead of yourself and screw it up, but at least you can right the ship." Nathan walked with them from the office to the elevator.

"We can." Martin pressed the button for the car. "Thanks."

"Thank you. It's rather nice to meet with clients that aren't assholes. Some of them really aren't fun," Nathan said. "We had to send one recently to collections and I hate that."

"I don't like it, either," Martin said as the doors opened. "But it's part of the game."

Justin shook hands with Nathan. "Thanks for the advice."

"Yes, thank you." Martin held back a beat while Justin entered the car. He dropped his voice to a whisper. "I'm sorry we didn't give your advice a chance before now. I'm sorry we didn't listen."

"You had to wake up. We all do." Nathan winked. "And now that you have, it'll sort out."

"You bet." He entered the car and waited for the doors to close. He waved, then sighed and turned to his brother. "Well, fuck."

"We did fuck." Justin leaned on the wall. "We can't be too forward, but we have to get her attention."

"We overstepped by shadowing her." He scratched his forehead. "So we go more lowkey and romance her."

"What the fuck do I know about romance?" Justin started forward when the doors opened. He didn't seem to care about Martin's answer.

Martin waited until they were in the car heading back to their offices before he spoke. "What do you mean, you don't know anything about romance? What about with Molly?"

Justin snorted. "Molly bought that stuff for herself and said I did it. I didn't know what to buy or what to pick out. I let her tell me."

"I thought you had a ring you'd planned to get."

"Nah. She had that one on her phone and sent me texts every so often as reminders. *Don't forget I want this one*, that kind of thing." Justin pulled a pair of panties from his pocket. "I did steal these from her."

"You're so romantic." He rolled his eyes. He should've known his cousin would have her underwear. "When?"

"When I hiked her skirt and made love to her on Nathan's desk." Justin grinned from ear to ear.

"You know he set that up for us to do that," Martin said. "He and I discussed it."

"You ass. You knew?" Justin shook his head and snorted. "I should've guessed you'd know. You're the brains of this."

"I'm not the brains of anything, but I thought it was smart to ask before we desecrated the office." He fiddled with the window button. "Honestly, I knew he wouldn't walk in because he understood what was going down. The thrill of being caught certainly propelled me, but I like walking the wire while having some safety nets in place."

"Makes sense." Justin leaned forward as the car stopped. "So what do we do?"

"Romance." He knew where they needed to go. "We'll give her the night, then send flowers tomorrow. Something sweet and understated so she doesn't feel overwhelmed, but shows that we're trying."

"So you're saying no big loud jewelry or rooms full of flowers?" Justin laughed and left the car. "No gifts of brand new sports cars?"

"No." Christ on a crutch. "Understated." He chased after his cousin into the office. Justin could create the best art and was brilliant with marketing, but he infuriated the hell out of him. If he wasn't careful, his cousin would send a fully loaded sports car to Chloe. Not that she might not need the car. For all he knew, she did. But she might not have anywhere to put it.

Justin stormed into his office. "What if we buy something she doesn't like? What if it's too smelly?"

"Whoa." He grasped Justin by the shoulders. "Slow down. You're freaking out over nothing. I'm not even sure what made you switch gears so fast. We send her something simple. A few roses and a card saying we're sorry."

"High-end roses," Justin said. "Not gas station ones."

"Of course." He wouldn't be so foolish to send something terrible. "When I dated Cindy, she liked quality and elegance. She knew both, when I didn't."

"So we get what she would've liked?" Justin shook his head, then shut the office door. "I don't want to make a copy of Cindy."

"That's not what I meant." He folded his arms and widened his stance. "We use what we already know she likes. Maybe we come up with something for her niece, too. You know? Charm them both? It can't hurt."

Justin considered what he'd said and didn't speak right away. "That makes sense. We want to show her we care about more than just getting with her."

"We want to make her part of our lives and that includes her niece right now. So we make sure they both feel special." He snapped his fingers. "I'll get the flowers ordered and you can handle the next part. Yeah?"

"Sounds good." Justin grinned. "We can do this."

"If we want more time with Chloe, then yes we will." He'd fallen in love with their curvy girl. She made his heart beat and made him realize he wanted another chance at forever. She could handle them both...if they gave her some time.

He returned to his own office and shut the door behind him. Being in his private space tended to ground him, but not today. He swore he'd dance right out of his skin. The whole situation with Chloe bothered him. He'd been too forward, no doubt. He'd checked up on her, knew her schedule and quite a bit of her history — all through his checking. He hadn't let her tell many of her stories. Hell, he hadn't even given her the chance to decide if this was what she wanted. He and Justin had simply decided for her that she'd be theirs.

Too forward.

He had to make this right. He'd told his cousin they'd figure it out and win her over, but beyond flowers, he wasn't sure how. The moment she found out he'd done so much research into her, she'd be pissed. She had to be angry that he and Nathan had orchestrated the play time at Sixxes.

Who could blame her for being upset?

The only way to fix this situation was to give her time. How best to do that? God, he had no idea. When he'd been with Cindy, she'd told him what to do. He'd had some ideas and she'd vetoed nearly all of them. A dull ache grew behind his eyes. Justin thought the relationship with Cindy had been so great. Not hardly. Most of the time, he'd simply followed her directions and kept his mouth shut. *Happy wife, happy life.*

Except he hadn't been nearly as happy as he'd portrayed. He'd done a lot of hiding. The less he fought with her, the better.

She'd demanded he buy lots of flowers. She liked jewelry. Once he had money, she wanted bigger jewelry. Better flowers. Lots of clothes.

Maybe Chloe would be the same way.

Maybe not.

He'd never know if he didn't try.

He opened his tablet and searched for florists. *Fuck.* What kind of flowers did she even like?

His phone rang and he glanced over at the number. He didn't recognize it, but something about it made him answer. "Hello?"

"This is your number then?"

He knew that voice. "Chloe?"

"It's me," she said. "I didn't want to call you, but I had to."

"Are you in trouble?" He'd just seen her, but still. "What's wrong?"

"Nothing's wrong necessarily, but I needed to talk to you."

"I'm here." He hit the button on his desk to lock the door. "What's wrong?" he repeated.

She didn't speak right away and he swore the call had been dropped. Instead of pushing, he waited.

"I needed to talk to you because I'm overwhelmed," she said. "I don't like crying, don't like being emotional and I hate being used."

"I know, babe." He'd been wrong to do just that.

"When I was a little girl, my parents paid me no attention. They were too busy fighting over the fact Dad had another family. His daughter, my older half-sister, Melinda, was the golden child for him. I was a reminder of his infidelity to my mother. Instead of being around when they fought, I sort of faded."

He sighed. He could understand that. He tended to try too hard to get attention while his cousin nabbed it all with his creativity.

"I'm only twenty-eight and my niece is fourteen. I never had the chance to be important because once I started coming into my own, my sister had Mad. I don't mind that she had her daughter. Madelin is wonderful, but she has a mother—not me."

"No, not you, but you're doing the best you can to step in and help her."

"I am." She laughed.

At least it sounded like a small laugh.

"After the divorce, I ran away from home a lot. I'd spend time at the clubs and out all hours of the night. I didn't want to be seen. I'd rather blend into the crowd and I did. I tried things I shouldn't have tried and went places I should've stayed away from because I was bored. I wanted to be anyone but me."

He waited a few beats before speaking. "What can I do to help? Just listen?"

"That does help. It also isn't bad that you're not yelling at me."

"Why? You had a reason for what you did," he said. "You don't deserve to be reprimanded. You need to be supported."

He could've sworn he heard a sob, but he wasn't certain.

"You deserve to be cherished."

"And you can do that for me?" she asked. "You and Justin?"

"We'd like to try," he murmured. "I know you're dealing with a lot. I know you're going through even more. The thing is, we'll work with you. If it means bringing your niece along, then it does. I'd love to take you to an upscale restaurant tonight, but mostly, what I want to do is hold you. To make you see everything is fine. It's going to be all right because you're not alone. You've got us."

"I do?"

"You do and if it means spanking you when the time shows up, then we do. If it means we wait for time, then we do. I don't mind. I know Justin doesn't, either. We want to make you happy."

She sighed and didn't speak again for a long moment. "Okay."

"Okay?"

"Yeah."

He paused. "How did you get my number? I don't mind you have it and I'm quite pleased you do. Keep it handy."

"I do the billing sometimes here at the office and your numbers are all in the file. I might have written it down."

"Good." He closed his eyes and massaged his forehead with his free hand. "Give us the chance and we'll make you happy."

"I know you will," she said. "Give me time and it'll sort out."

"Little steps."

"Little steps," she replied. She hung up, leaving him in silence.

For the first time since he'd left the legal office, he wasn't upset. Wasn't even stressed. She'd figured out a way to get through to him and make him feel better.

Maybe she did need time, but he'd give her what she wanted. More than that, he'd be there for her because she'd done the same for him.

Chapter Nine

Chloe spent the next three days with Madelin. She cheered her niece at the football game during the halftime show, went to the joint band venture pitting various high school bands against each other for the honor of the best band, and even had girls' night on Sunday with Madelin and Kindra. She loved every second with Madelin and marveled at the way Madelin and her friend interacted. Like an old married couple. They understood each other. They laughed and teased each other, but still cared. They finished the other's sentences.

She longed to have that kind of a friendship.

Her sister had no idea the kinship between these girls. Maybe they were practicing and fumbling through life and love or maybe it was something more, but they respected each other.

As she left work Monday, her phone rang. Not Martin, but her sister. She switched the phone to speaker and climbed behind the wheel of her car. "Yes?"

"I saw you made it to the game."

"I did," she said and pulled out of her parking spot. "I didn't know you were there." She'd looked for Melinda, but the crowd size had made locating her difficult.

"I stayed out of sight."

"Why?" she asked. "Are you afraid that if she sees you, she might realize her mother does care?"

"She knows I care."

"Please." She groaned and wove through traffic. She'd put up with this garbage for long enough. Her niece deserved better. "You might think she knows, but she needs to hear it. You think you show it, but you don't. She likes her friend, but she's fourteen. She's still figuring her life out. If you encourage her and back off getting angry with her over her friendships, then you might see she'll give you a chance. She might let you in. She's aching to have her mother be a mother, not the traumatic authoritarian."

"That's what you think I am?"

"I think you're afraid of screwing this up and you're trying too hard to not do that, all while fucking it all up. Stop worrying about how you'll mess up and let the mess happen. For Christ's sake, she's a good kid who is in that weird time between being a kid and adult. The world is big and scary, but it's not impossible if you stop being so hard on her. Sure, you can keep her in line, but in line doesn't mean being overbearing."

"I see."

Her sister didn't give a shit. Of course. She'd been talking to herself. "Mel, you really do need to take this all to heart."

"I'm sure I do."

"She's a good kid."

"She is," Melinda said. "I'm worried she'll get out of control."

"Like me?" she asked and winced.

"Yes."

"So you let her run off to live with me?"

"I had no choice. That's where she wanted to go and I knew she'd be safe," Melinda said. "But I also know you're not always the best influence."

"Because of my past?"

"Because of how you behaved in school, after school. You're not married. You're not even in a relationship, so you're showing her that it's okay to be single."

She growled. "It is okay."

"Is it? There's no structure."

She sighed as she pulled into her parking spot in the second row of the building lot. "You're right. I don't have structure. Don't have a job, my own income, car or anything else. I'm just flailing in the wind."

"You know what I mean."

She did and it wasn't right. "That's just it. Mel, you're treating me the way you're treating her. She's at that tender age, but I'm not a child. I'm not steering her toward the same direction I went into, but I'm also not going to push her in any direction. I'm letting her figure out what she wants—within reason."

"I know you are and I don't like it, but you're in charge right now because she looks up to you."

She knew that. "What do you want to do?"

"I want my daughter to come home, but she doesn't want to. She says she likes living there. She says she's happy and her grades are up."

"That's not what she's telling me. She says you're trying to get rid of her." She probably should look at Mad's grades, but she wasn't the parent, so she might not be able to.

Her phone buzzed and she glanced down at the screen. Martin. She really wanted to have a night with him and Justin tonight.

"You're not listening to me."

She snapped her attention back to her sister. "You're right. I'm not. I have other things to do tonight and to make sure she gets her homework done, so I need to go."

"You're going to hang up?"

"Yes." She did just that and ended that call to speak to Martin. "Hi."

"Hi, babe. How's things? Was the game a good one?" he asked.

She appreciated that he'd shown interest in her life. He didn't seem afraid of bringing up her niece or what they'd done. "The game was a blowout and our team lost, but that's to be expected. It's a lot of younger players and they're still learning the game. The band sounded fantastic and Mad played her heart out. They had another concert the next day and her school came in third of fifteen. Sunday, we watched movies with her friend Kindra."

"Wonderful. Is she adjusting?"

"She is." She laughed. This conversation was so much easier than with her sister. "She had a great time this weekend and she seems happier than I've seen her in a long time."

"Good to hear," he said. "And you. Are you still wearing the collar?"

She shifted in her seat and swore her cheeks were on fire. Heat pooled between her legs. The sheer mention of the collar reminded her of their times together. She longed to have his hands on her ass. Justin nipping at her throat. Both men pushing into her at the same time. She swallowed a moan.

"I'm going to take that as a yes."

She whimpered. Her nipples beaded and the temperature in the car rose a hundred degrees. "It's a yes."

"Yes, what?"

She loved this part of the game. "Yes, sir."

"Good girl."

Pleasure slipped through her veins. "I've been good, sir. I haven't masturbated since we played. Haven't gotten off at all."

"I'm proud of you and will reward you when we're together again."

"Thank you, sir." She hadn't totally entered into a contract with them. Hadn't signed anything or even come up with a formal contract, but she wanted to. She longed to be the third in their triad. Silly, really. Things had just started and could go sideways so fast. But she didn't care.

"I want to see you," he said. "Soon. Tonight?"

"Tonight?" She left the car and grabbed her purse, then locked the vehicle. "I don't know if I can. Mad will be home."

"Bring her along."

She paused. "What?" That wasn't possible. Bringing her niece along on a date? How in the hell was she going to explain that?

"What do you mean? I thought we'd go to the Skee Ball Shack. She'll find out eventually about us, but that doesn't mean she can't find out this way that we're friends. We all go out for pizza, wings and those games. We have fun awhile and get along. You get out, she has a good night and we can all lose ourselves while having fun."

"You keep saying the word fun."

"I want you to relax."

She fumbled for her keys, then stuffed them in the lock and twisted it. The door opened and she crinkled her nose. "What did you have in mind? What time?" She didn't see Madelin, but she smelled the pungent scent of teen body spray. "Can you text me? I have to deal with something."

"Madelin?"

"I think so. Talk later." She hung up, regretting that she had to hang up so fast, then put her purse and phone down. "Mad?" She wandered through the apartment to the guest room. No Madelin. The bathroom light caught her attention. She pivoted and ran headlong into the offensive scent.

"Sorry." Madelin waved her arms through the air. "I'm sorry."

"What are you doing?" She coughed and waved her arms. "What are you spraying?"

"I tried this new body spray, but it was a joke. Sam gave me a bullshit bottle and I thought it was real, so I sprayed it, but the button got stuck and it smells like ass." Madelin turned the vent fan up and waved her arms toward the windows. "He lied to me and I thought it was real. I thought he liked me." She stopped moving and stared at Chloe. Her eyes widened. As if realization dawned in her mind, tears slipped down her cheeks.

"Come out here." She tugged her niece to the front room, then the patio to the fresh outside air. Madelin threw herself into Chloe's arms and sobbed. Chloe sighed and held on to her. "Get your breath and calm down, then tell me what happened. Tell me. I'm here."

Madelin sobbed a bit longer then stilled. "Kindra and I made a pact to find boyfriends, so she and Corey are a couple. Corey said Sam liked me and I like him, so I asked him if he wanted to be together…whatever that means. Anyway, he gave me this cologne and said I'd like it. He said to spray a bunch of it and had this strange smile on his face. I did and now it stinks."

"Would he tease you?"

"I don't know."

"Did he seem like he liked you, too?"

"Kind of?"

She nodded. "I don't know if he did or didn't. He seems to have played a terrible prank on you, but you know what? When he calls tonight, we're not going to think about him. We're going to give ourselves time."

"We are?" Madelin stared at her with smudged makeup and tears all over her cheeks. "Are you sending me home?"

"No." That was the last thing her niece needed right now. "We're going to go out." At least she hoped so. If Martin and Justin didn't come through, then she'd have a plan of her own.

"Yeah?" Madelin nodded. "I'd like that."

"No phones. Just girls tonight, unless my friends want to go out, then we'll have a friends' night and have a good time. How does the Skee Ball Shack sound?"

"I'd love it." She finally smiled. "Why do boys have to be complicated?"

"I don't know." She wasn't sure why her sister had to be, too. They'd never be one gigantic happy family, but they had to learn to get along. Jesus. Her sister had to be a parent. Madelin deserved a real mom who cared. She guided her niece back into the apartment and kicked out of her high-heeled shoes. She checked her phone. Sure enough, there was a message from Martin. A car would be there at six-forty-five to pick them up and take them in style to the Skee Ball Shack.

She shook her head. He understood. He and Justin got what she was going through.

"What's up?" Madelin returned in different clothes and her hair in a ponytail. "Did you change your mind?"

"No." She sighed and put the phone down. She wasn't sure how Martin knew where she lived, but she also didn't care. He'd find out eventually. "We have about twenty minutes to get dressed and ready. The bigger surprise is about to arrive." She rushed into her bedroom to change from her work dress into a pair of jeans and a loose blouse. Her thoughts turned to when she'd played with Justin and lost her panties to him. That man. He'd made her go the rest of the day indecent under her dress.

She could be indecent and secretly please them for the remainder of the night tonight as well.

She donned the jeans and located a pair of socks, then one of her lacy bras and her blouse before putting them all on.

"Are we taking a limo?" Madelin came into the room. "I'm glad you're dressed because there's a guy walking up to the door and he just arrived in a limo."

"Limo?" *Oh brother*. They'd have to bring something so fantastic. She grabbed her boots and rushed to the door. When she peeked through the window, she noticed Martin on the doorstep. She twisted the knob. "A limo?"

He grinned and rocked on his heels. "I thought we'd go in style. Is Madelin ready?"

"She will be." She shook her head, then put on her boots. "Is Justin in the car?"

"Waiting patiently. He's not good at patient, so hurry up." Martin touched the collar. "By the way, are you decent?"

"Me?" she murmured. "I might have gone without to please you."

"Oh?" His eyes flashed. "Nothing?"

"Nothing." She leaned on the doorframe. "So you'll have to think about it."

"Naughty. You just told me you'd been good." He nodded once. "You must be Madelin. I'm Martin."

Madelin grinned. "This is the guy you were seeing?" She elbowed Chloe. "He's hot."

"He can hear you," Chloe replied. She wanted to melt into the floor and hide. "Oh boy."

"I can, but it's okay. I'm pleased to meet you." Martin stepped out of the way. "Ladies, the chariot awaits and we're going to have a great time. Anyone for Skee Ball Shack?"

"I thought..." Madelin snorted. "You knew he was coming over, didn't you?"

"I did." She sighed and grabbed her keys, purse and phone. "After you." She waited for Madelin to go through the doorway first, then closed the door behind her and locked up. When she turned back around, Justin was out of the car. He stood next to the vehicle grinning. He touched his pocket, then tipped his head as if he knew she'd gone without.

That man!

Madelin practically skipped to the car. "This is so cool. I never thought I'd get to ride in one. Mom would shit."

Martin's brows rose, but he said nothing. Justin laughed. "My mother wasn't big on extravagances, either," he said. "She liked being frugal."

"Extravagance?" Madelin snorted and shook her head. "She'd be jealous I'm doing this and not her. She'd be angry Auntie Chloe is, too. Mom's supposed to be the star. Everyone revolves around her."

"Everything," Chloe said. "The entire world does."

Justin said nothing and climbed into the back of the car, followed by Madelin. Martin touched Chloe's shoulder, causing her to stop. She glanced back and paused.

"Yes?" She slid her hand over his chest. "Sir?"

"I get your pain, babe. It's not okay to be in pain, but it's okay to share it." He kissed her. "Share it with us and have fun. Tonight is about being free and having a good time."

"I will." She needed a night to relax. One without and problems where she and Madelin could forget. "Thank you."

"You're welcome." He waited for her to settle in the back of the car before joining them. He sat beside her and Justin faced them. Madelin toyed with the bar.

"It's dry." She frowned. "I thought this fancy thing would have lots of bad things." Madeline grinned, then fiddled with the sunroof button.

"Don't do that." She hated when she switched into parental mode, but the last thing she needed was to pay for the repairs to a limo that cost more than she made in a year.

"It's okay. Martin plays with it when he's bored," Justin said. "She can't hurt it."

A likely story. She folded her hands on her lap. "I've never been in a limo."

"No?" Justin winked. "Well now you have."

Martin opened the console and withdrew four bottles of soda. "Want one?"

Madelin's eyes lit up. "Please?"

He handed her one. "Chloe?"

"Thank you." She accepted the bottle. The drive to the shack wasn't that long, but she didn't mind. She enjoyed the time and being with these men. They made her feel wanted and warm. They brought out excitement and got her to think. She was protected. Not a puppet or a plaything. Just a woman who needed to be loved.

Holy shit.

Loved.

She paused. That's what she'd been missing. Not that they were offering that to her. Maybe not yet, and maybe not ever. She might not be their forever, but she could be their right now and have a good time.

They could come to love her.

Could.

She shifted her gaze between Martin and Justin. They were handsome together. Felt like heaven when they made love to her. Different in their own ways, but the same. She wanted to feel them moving within her at the same time. Fucking her and making her skin hot. Making her crazy with need. Tied to their bed or spanked under their hands. She'd give herself over to them without a second thought. They made her sing. Made her fly.

Tonight, she'd have a good time with them and exist. She'd find out what being cherished would be like. She'd be happy.

Not the normal girl, but the fun one. The one they desired. The one in her heart.

The woman she'd always known she could be.

Herself.

Chapter Ten

Justin spent the next three hours laughing, eating and playing games with Martin, Chloe and Madelin. He liked being part of a family again, even if the family was of his own making. Madelin cracked him up. He'd forgotten what it was like to be with others who cared. Sure, he'd spent plenty of time with Martin growing up. They were like brothers. But eventually they had to separate—Martin lived in a different house with parents who paid attention.

He finished his pizza slice and pushed the plate away. Chloe sat beside him a moment.

"Hey." She sighed and tucked wispy locks of her hair back into place. "I haven't had this much fun in so long. I don't usually have the money for extras like this."

"What? The tickets?" He'd have to rectify that. She deserved to have a few nice things. If she wanted tickets, she could have them. Or shoes, dresses, clothes, or even jewelry. He wanted to pamper her.

"I try to come up with a supper out, or at least takeout on Fridays for her, but I don't have the extra to do fun things like this," Chloe said. "The club was a luxury I don't usually get, either. If Darinda hadn't helped, I wouldn't have gone."

"I get it." He slipped his arm around her. "But you don't have to worry about that. If you need extra, say something."

"I should work for it, not be handed anything."

"True, but everyone can use a little help from time to time." He kissed her cheek. "I like Mad. She's fun and I like the way you light up when you're out with her. You're a good mother to her, you know. You've got the knack."

"Do I?" She blushed. "I always feel like I'm screwing up."

"Nah."

"You have no idea. I feel like the advice I give her is ignored. I've always been in the background. I'm not the one who has kids. I'm the one who screws up and gets messed up." She shook her head and leaned forward. "Do you understand what I mean?"

"More than you think." He rubbed her back. "When I was a kid, my mother and father weren't interested in me. They were so big into their careers and I was an afterthought. I spent more time with Martin. Nothing I did was important enough. Nothing I accomplished was good enough. They simply didn't have time for me. I always thought they didn't want me."

She met his gaze. "You get it and I'm sorry you do. You deserved better than that."

"Which is why I worked so hard to make myself better. I gave up trying to impress them and decided to impress myself. What could I do to make the world better? To be creative? That's how I moved on." He petted her hair. "You can, too. You are, because you're making her life better."

She stared at him. "I hadn't thought about that."

"She looks up to you."

"She seems to like you and Martin." She nodded to them playing a game of basketball. "She doesn't open up much."

"The limo helped." He'd used it as an icebreaker many times with clients. "What are you doing Friday?"

"Working."

"Ah." He nodded. "If you don't mind, I'll talk to Nathan and get you the day off. We'd like to play and I understand you're hesitant to while your niece is around, so…a day off work while she's at school and time to play might do you good."

She swept her gaze over him. "You're asking me out?"

"Uh-huh. I mean, I'd also include some negotiations. Some spanking." He toyed with a lock of her hair. "Some play. Some fucking hot sex. Some time being naked and holding you."

She shivered. "I'd love that."

"I know you're not wearing underwear."

"I'm not."

"I knew it." He slid his hand down her back to her waistline and slipped one finger beneath the denim. "Soft and silky, just like I knew it would be. I can't wait to kiss every inch of you, including that sweet pussy. You're like wine. You flow in my system."

"Do I?" She parted her lips, but her words came out in a whisper. "Me?"

"You. I want to part those thighs and sip from you."

"Yes." She cleared her throat, then sat up straighter. "They're coming over."

"Don't want Martin to know?" he whispered.

"Nope. Don't want her to hear us." She smoothed her jeans, then stood. "Did you have fun?"

"We've got enough tickets to cash in for something." Madelin pulled a wad of folded tickets from her pocket. "This guy knows how to shoot hoops."

"I saw." Chloe folded her hands again. "What are you going to cash them in for?"

"I don't know." Madelin grasped her arm. "Come with me and help me choose."

Before Justin could say anything, Chloe ran off with Madelin. Justin tossed the used napkins onto the pile of plates, then stacked the remains of their dinner in a pile. "I've never seen anyone get so into her skee ball."

"Yeah?" Martin folded his arms and widened his stance. "So. Did you ask her about Friday?"

"I hate having to schedule time like this, but yeah. I did and she liked it," Justin said. He watched her while she and Madelin spent the tickets. "I can't wait to have her in my arms. Between us. I'm dying for a scene and she's the only one who can make it happen. Who can make me whole. She's the one we need."

"I agree." Martin pushed the pile of plates across the table. "She's aching to be loved, you know."

"I do."

"So we plan the day on Friday and call Nathan to set it up. I don't want her docked, but I do want her on our terms," Justin said. "We've made everything else work. We can make this work, too."

"You're so cocky." Martin laughed, then left a few dollars on the table for the tip. "We gave her the thing she needed most tonight. We gave her a night to forget and have a good time."

"We did." Justin paid the bill before joining them all at the counter. He'd had the time of his life, too, but everything had to come to an end and the real world needed his attention. Friday, he'd have the time of his life.

* * * *

Friday morning, Justin wandered into the playroom. He'd ensured the space had everything they'd need for the day. The toys mattered. He needed to make this experience one she'd never forget and for her to see they belonged together.

Martin strolled into the room. "I'm picking her up in a few moments. Do you want anything else brought in?"

He surveyed the room. *Paddles, vibrators, plugs, straps...* "We're ready."

"Good." Martin turned on his heel and left.

He hesitated a moment, then raced after his cousin. "Let me pick her up. You always handle those details. Let me do it." He appreciated his cousin's desire to control things, but this time, he should have some hand in what was going on.

"You want to?"

"Yes." He took the keys from Martin. "It's my turn." He'd always given over control to Martin. Most of the time, this worked for them both, but right now, this had to be his job. He needed to show her he was serious about being with her.

"Then by all means." Martin tipped his head, then waved. "Enjoy."

"I will." He had plenty of ideas as to what he wanted to do on the way home. He hurried out to the garage, then behind the wheel of his favorite car. The vehicle offered great handling on the road and luxury features, while feeling like a sports car, but having a bit more room like a sedan. He needed that bit of room for what he had in mind for the three of them.

Within a few moments, he was speeding across town to her apartment. The moment he parked at her sidewalk, his heart hammered. He'd been waiting for this chance for so long. Waiting for her. He hadn't known she was the one, but the minute he'd seen her, he knew. His heart knew when he played with her. The dancing, the smiles, the way she felt against him — it was all right.

Chloe strode down the walkway, clad in a trench coat. Her patent leather shoes caught the light. She yanked open the car door and slid onto the front seat. "Hi. This is some car. Is it bulletproof?"

"Hello, beautiful." He reached over and patted her thigh. "Look at you. I need a bulletproof car to bring you home because I'll be fighting off the other men dying to take you away."

"Take me? They might beg you to take me, not the other way around." She nodded. "Am I okay? I tried to listen to what Martin asked for."

"You've done well." He paused. "You tend to feel less than worthy, don't you?"

"Maybe." She shrugged, but he knew the signs of denial.

"You do, but you don't have to feel that way with us. You're very much who we want." He moved the coat aside. "No pants?"

"Nope." She opened the coat, then shrugged it off her shoulders. Instead of a bra or dress, she wore nothing but a strand of pearls and stockings. She rubbed her bare arms and whimpered.

"Problem?" Not for him. Good fucking God, he loved the view. "You're goose pimpled."

"I am. I'm not used to being nude like this — not that I don't like it. I do." She shifted in her seat and faced him. "He insisted on the pearls."

"I'm glad he did and I'm glad you're being this free. You're gorgeous." He slid his hand up her thigh to her pussy. The scent of her perfume raced around the car. The sheer excitement of being around her sent blood rushing to his dick. He traced the line of her smooth pussy lips.

Her whimpers and the softness of her skin as well as the slight glint of her liquid excitement encouraged him. Emboldened by her, he eased one finger between her sweet lips. Her cream slicked his fingers. Christ, he'd never get enough of that heat.

"Do you want me?" he asked and massaged her outer lips.

"I do," she said, her voice gravelly. She shifted in her seat, moving lower and opening her legs more. "More, please?"

He couldn't tell her no. "What do you want to do?" Endorphins raced through his system. He rode high on adrenaline. The faster they got home, the faster he could have her surrounding him. He needed to feel the softness of her hair, feel the thrum of her body on his and taste her kiss. Mostly, he needed that kiss.

"I want to be yours, sir. Yours and Martin's." She parted her thighs farther. "I want to belong to you while you fuck me, use me and make me scream. Spank me, cuff me. I need it all because it's from you."

"Then you'll have all those things and more. You'll have pretty much whatever you want, babe." He kept his hand between her legs, but used his free hand to awkwardly shift the car into gear and backed out of the spot. As he drove across town, he toyed with her pussy. He moved his finger in and out of her, smearing cream around her sensitive skin.

"Oh, sir."

He loved the way that sounded on her lips. "You're wearing the collar." He hadn't missed that detail. From the moment Martin had put the platinum strand around her throat, the chain had stayed there. It looked so perfect against her skin.

"I am." She shivered and grasped the armrest. "I'm here to be yours."

Her inner walls fluttered against his finger. Close to orgasm? He twisted his digit to change the way he touched her and slow the climax.

"You're so mean." She moaned. "I'm so close."

"I know you are, but you can't come yet. What if I want more than just for you to be mine? Ours?" he asked and turned into the side street. "What if I want love from you?" He speared a second finger into her cunt. Her heat filled him up. He needed more. Needed devotion. Wanted craving. Never wanted her to go.

"I…" She writhed on him, shoving his fingers deeper into her body. When he curled his digit into her G-spot, she cried out.

Yeah, that was the place. He caressed the tender flesh, making her writhe again and moan. He loved having this power and knew how he'd use it. Just for her and for making them all whole. To get her off, but also bring her closer to him and his cousin. To prove the triad worked well.

"Yes, babe. Ride me." He sped up the driveway to the garage and parked in the usual spot. The tires screeched as he stopped and the scent of burnt rubber filtered lightly through the air. When he turned off the car, he backed the seat up as far as he could. He'd waited long enough for this and wasn't about to wait another second. "Come here." He slid his fingers from her body, missing her heat and the tenderness of her cunt.

She trembled as she looked at him. "Sir." Her nipples beaded and the blush crept over her chest.

His heartbeat hammered in his ears. Nothing else mattered and the world around them seemed to melt away as he looked into her eyes. He opened his pants, shoved them slightly down his thighs, then withdrew his cock. The scene would happen, but he needed sated first. The move was demanding, but he didn't care. This kind of pleasure couldn't be contained. "Come here." He reached for her, then guided her onto his lap. He pushed into her in one thrust. He'd fucked in plenty of cars, but never this one and never like this. "Need you."

Chloe bounced on him, her breasts jiggling in his face. "Sir." She grasped his shoulders. The pearls swayed on her upper chest and added to the beauty and elegance of the moment.

Christ, he loved this. He buried his face in her chest, then sucked on one of her nipples. When she cried out again, he bit. She tasted like sin and sex. She smelled wonderful and he trailed his nose along the swell of her breast. The shriek of ecstasy spurred him on. He pulled her down harder on his dick. At the same time, she dug her nails into his shoulders. The bit of pain added to the moment.

She leaned down and kissed him. "Sir. Fuck me, sir."

"Mine." He grasped her breast, then swatted her ass. The crack echoed in the car. The sounds of her panting overruled everything else. When she kissed him, he opened to her. The second he slid his tongue across hers, he deepened the connection. She'd be the one he couldn't forget.

She writhed more on his cock. "Sir." Her head lolled on her shoulders and she backed into the steering wheel. The horn blared. She lurched and smashed into him as the sound filled the air. "Sorry."

"Don't be." He ground his teeth together. Nothing could hold back this moment. "Fuck." He surged into her and the quick orgasm rocked into his body. The good feelings overwhelmed him and took the edge off the situation. He didn't want to screw this up. Wanted her to feel like a queen.

"I'm close, sir." She moaned again. "I…" She tightened around him and tipped her head back. She slid one hand up to her breast and plucked her nipple.

Fuck, he wanted to watch that again. He loved her freedom with her body. "Don't you dare come until we're all three together."

"What?" She snapped her eyes open and her lips parted, but she said nothing else.

He couldn't stop if his life depended on it. He welcomed the orgasm and moved with abandon. For a moment the world seemed to move at half speed. He felt every ripple and flutter in her pussy. The tightness pushed him over the edge. When he looked into her eyes, he knew she was the one. He tumbled headlong into orgasm as he came and filled her pussy with his seed.

"Sir." She tightened around him again and bunched her hands. "Yes, sir." She trembled, no doubt on the same edge she'd pushed him over.

"That's right." He held her fast to his groin and stared into her eyes again. He saw forever there. He noticed the light and life he'd always hoped he could possess if he had her. If *they* had her. She was the one they needed. The missing piece. "Hold on to me. I won't let you go."

Chloe tucked against him and panted. "We need to go inside, but I don't know if I can hold myself up, sir."

"I won't let anything hurt you." He glanced up and noticed Martin in the doorway. "We've got you." Well, fuck. He'd get an earful for starting without his cousin, but the need had been too great. He regretted nothing.

"I know you do." She curled against him and sighed. "I trust you."

"Don't trust me for long. We're about to be interrupted."

Martin opened the door. "You've started without me."

"Sir." She sat up and grasped Justin's shirt. "I..."

"It's fine, babe. You're beautiful." Martin said and held out his hand. He laughed as he helped her from the car. Instead of allowing her to walk, he scooped her into his arms. "As for you, zip up and follow me." He turned his attention back to Chloe. "Seeing you fucking him, and so free like that, pleased your sir. I loved it and want to see more. Yes?"

"Yes." She tucked against him and held on.

Justin grinned. He'd worried they might be making a mistake, but now he knew the truth. They'd found their girl and it was high time they took control. Never let it be said they didn't get what they wanted.

And she was who they wanted.

Chapter Eleven

Chloe hung onto Martin as he carried her into the house. She'd never been to their home and had no idea what she was walking...or rather being carried into. When she looked up, she nearly gasped. She'd never seen a side room so luxurious. Wood paneling, marble counters and everything tucked away. Even plants!

He carried her to the kitchen and placed her on the counter. The chilly granite cooled her ass. She fiddled with her hands, trying to figure out what to do with herself. Tuck her legs under her? Request her coat? Sit still?

At the same time, she embraced the feeling of safety and security. She'd just done something totally out of her character and she'd loved it. Now she was with two men she had no business being with and loved that, too. She'd been so dirty and free.

"You're shivering." Martin scooped a burgundy garment from the other counter. "Put this on."

"What is it?" She allowed him to slip the silky fabric around her. A robe.

He arranged the robe to give her coverage. "There. That's better."

"Don't want to see me naked?" She understood that. She'd been told she was too curvy for her own good. Too much body and she should whittle it down a bit.

"Who said that?" He frowned, then rested his hands on his hips. "Are you hungry?"

"Huh?" She'd heard him, but she needed the words repeated. "I'm sorry?"

"Are you hungry? It's nearly ten in the morning, I don't know if you've eaten or if you're thirsty, but you've been out in the car expending a lot of energy with Justin. It stands to reason you'd be hungry and thirsty." He rested his hip against the counter. "You're permitted to be both. You should be taken care of, and well at that."

She fumbled with his words. *Holy shit. This isn't real.* Couldn't be. "May I have a glass of water?" She didn't want to bring attention to her curves. If she ate, then they might notice.

"You may." He poured a glass of water in a fancy crystal glass, then handed it to her. "The robe is to allow you to warm up and the food and water is for you to gear up for what we're going to do next. Why wouldn't I offer these? You seem perplexed, and I am, so enlighten me."

She sipped the water, then held on to the glass with both hands. God, she didn't want to drop the thing. It probably cost half of her paycheck. "First, this is expensive and I don't deserve expensive. Second, I'm here for a scene. That doesn't include food and drink. It's sex and play." She drank more of the water and realized how thirsty she'd become. Hell, she was ravenous. "Besides, for the day, you own me."

"No." He shook his head. "Even if we do a contract, it's not for all day. It's for while we're in the bedroom, and I refuse to own anyone. That's another reason why I offered you food. We need to talk before we do anything."

"Understood." She flexed her fingers around the glass.

"Uh-huh." He stared at her. "You do deserve expensive — or cheap — or whatever you want. You're a gem and we're honored to know you. And yes, so you're here for a scene, but that doesn't mean you don't deserve human decency. I'm hungry and I can't imagine you're not." He pivoted and opened the fridge. A moment later, he withdrew a plate of fruit and cheese. He nodded to her.

"Whoa." She hated sounding so lowbrow.

"Have some." He put the platter next to her. "All you want."

"Thank you." She nibbled on a piece of cheddar cheese and reminded herself not to take too much.

"You're permitted to eat. Good God. If you're hungry, then eat. It's sexy when a woman eats." He tucked a lock of her hair behind her ear. "Babe, we don't want you to starve because you think we want something we're not looking for. You caught our attention because of who you are. We love your curves, your smile, the way you laugh and your tenacity. Don't lose that."

She hesitated. "I won't."

"Good." He picked up a handful of grapes. "Where in the hell is my cousin?"

"Right here." Justin rushed into the room. "Fuck. We got a call from Dockery. There's been some issues at the house and he was pissed. I don't know what was screwed up, but I had to call Denes and it turns out they broke the counter. They're paying for it instead of us, since they dropped it, but still. It's putting the job behind schedule. I think I smoothed it over, but the way Dockery made it sound, he tried to call you and you weren't answering so he called me."

Martin crooked his brow. "My phone's right there and it never lit up."

She nibbled on another piece of cheese. She had no idea what all they'd discussed, but it sounded important. "Why'd they drop it?" she asked, then wished she'd kept her mouth shut. "Sorry."

"No, no." Martin picked up more grapes. "We don't actually do the work. Justin designs the concept and I have people to hire the crews. I oversee the work, but it's more of popping in and ensuring the work is being done. I trust my crews and most of them are great. Every so often, we have an issue."

"Oh." She stole a strawberry from the platter. "Sounds interesting. All I do is billing and filing. They have enough clients and junior partners that we're always busy. Some days all I do is coding for billing."

"That's better than me," Justin said. "I hate coding anything."

"You hate paperwork," Martin replied. "But someone has to do it."

"You don't have people to do it?" She ate the strawberry, then picked up another. "They farm out to us a lot of work. Honestly, the brothers don't practice that much law. I guess if you've got people to do it, then let them. Or you only take specific clients."

"They're particular." Martin rested his elbows on the counter. "We hadn't told you what we do, or asked what you do."

"Billing and filing. Bringing the paperwork in to you all was sort of a fluke." She paused, then toyed with her glass. "No, it was probably set up. I don't put anything past them now. Or you."

"You're not wrong." Martin winked. "We might have had a hand in it. I know it's shitty because you don't want someone pulling the strings, but we wanted to see you and when we found out you were there, we jumped at the chance."

Justin plucked grapes and three slices of cheese from the platter. "Speak for yourself. You told me it was a surprise, so I didn't know, but I'm damn glad you were there and the surprise was set up."

She swore she blushed again and averted her gaze as she ate the berry. "Thanks."

"Speaking of making things happen and surprises, you're here as a bit of a gift. We wanted to give you a few hours without cares or worries. Just play and fun." Martin's eyes shimmered. "We also wanted to extend the opportunity to create a contract with us."

She sucked in a ragged breath, thankful she wasn't trying to eat anything. "Oh?" A contract with them? Only play with Martin and Justin? Yes, please. "How so?"

"Well, that's where we negotiate." Justin popped another piece of cheese into his mouth. "We realize you've got your niece, so it's complicated for you, but we'd like you to be our only partner in the bedroom."

"The only partner out of the bedroom, too," Martin said. "Our girl for events and quiet nights in. We'll provide you with clothes, shoes, jewelry, whatever you need for a night out, plus give you an allowance. When you stay here, you'll sleep with us."

"And when we play, you're ours to use. Spanking, toys, bondage, blindfolds and you'll give in to both of us, even if it means we both make love to you at the same time," Justin said. "We respect you and want to make you happy. Want to see you fly. We trust you'll tell us if you've been pushed too far or aren't interested."

"We'll take care of you," Martin said. "But you have to agree and you're welcome to negotiate. What are your terms?"

She exhaled and considered their words. They were offering her the world and with the consideration of her situation with her niece. Most men would simply demand and expect her to follow through. "I see."

"It's your turn to speak. We don't make every one of the rules." Justin tipped his head. "Chloe?"

"Well…" She had to think this through and explain herself clearly. "I trust you to take care of me and I trust you to respect me. I expect nothing less. I accept your terms for play and will happily use my safe word if I feel I've been pushed too far. I have no problem with speaking up if I'm not comfortable. I'm your girl and I will do my best to make you happy. I don't require tons of clothes or any of the other material things. My biggest request is respect." *And love.*

Not yet. It was too soon to ask for that.

Martin nodded and Justin ate another piece of cheese.

She sat up a bit straighter and folded her hands on her lap. "You're not going to require a specific time each week, or so many hours? Or that I sleep here at least one night a week?"

"How can we do that when you have to care for Madelin?" Martin asked. "We want you here all the time, but she needs you more."

She wasn't sure about that, but she respected their rationale.

"Besides, we'll figure out when to get together. If we're meant to play often, we will. If not, then we'll come up with something else," Justin said. "There will be times when she needs you and we'll have to wait. Then there will be times when we have longer hours and won't be able to make a scene happen when we all desire."

She respected that. "Makes sense."

"And since you're already wearing our collar, we'll keep it locked as a sign you're ours. If you want a formal contract, we'll have that drawn up," Justin said.

"Who'll do that?" she blurted. She didn't want someone else knowing about what they were doing — not yet. At least not in the bedroom. That was their personal business.

"Me," Martin said. "I'm not farming that out, as you put it."

She sighed and rubbed her forehead. "Good." She couldn't handle the embarrassment of someone else knowing what was going on. People knowing she was dating them was one thing, but people knowing that she liked being spanked was another.

"What do you think?" Justin asked. "You'll be our girl and we'll be your sirs in the bedroom. Outside of that, you're our babe and you can call us whatever you want."

"You're the queen of our world and the only one in both our bedroom and playroom," Martin said. "No one else. What do you think?"

She nodded and couldn't hold back the smile as she sipped the last of her water. "I agree." The robe slipped off her shoulder and she didn't try to cover back up. "Sirs, I'd like to play." She wanted to see the playroom and feel their hands on her body. To give herself over to them.

Right now.

"Yes, babe." Martin put the empty glass in the sink, then returned the platter to the fridge. He scooped her into his arms, then placed her on her feet, but kept his arm around her. "Tell us your safe word."

She clasped her hands together at the small of her back. "My safe word is stop, but I don't wish to use it."

"You will if you feel you need to and you will speak whenever you wish, yes?" Justin asked. He loped his arm around her waist.

"I will." Her heart hammered and heat pooled in her belly. "I'm ready for whatever you have in mind."

"Very well." Martin led the way through the house. "Come along."

She didn't bother to take in her surroundings. Instead, she rushed to keep up with him. She'd lost her shoes in the car and the carpet was soft under her feet. When he stopped, she nearly collided with his back.

She drank in the view of the array of toys and apparatuses. "This is your home?"

"It is." Martin grinned. "Could be yours, too."

She had to be dreaming. She could live here? She hadn't even looked at the rest of the house, but they wanted to keep her around that long. "I want to submit to you."

"Good girl." Justin helped her out of the robe. "Warm enough?"

"I am." She clasped her hands together at the small of her back. Her skin prickled with anticipation.

Justin walked around her three times, then stopped in front of her. "You've pleased us. So sweet and smart." He tweaked her nipple. "So receptive."

She bit back a groan. She loved being pinched and swatted. "How can I please you?"

"Bend over the bed. Ass in the air." Martin folded his arms and widened his stance. "Now."

She loved that tone. Chloe scrambled onto the bed. She rested on her hands and knees, then opened her legs. Being in this position added to her vulnerability.

"Good girl." Justin stopped in front of her and winked. "You need some jewelry." He produced a pair of nipple clips. Bells tingled from the rings on them. Heat engulfed her pussy. She longed to press her knees together to quell the desire. Justin pinched her left nipple, then affixed the clip.

She winced at the pinch. The teeth bit into her skin and sent a rush of desire through her body. "Thank you, sir. May I have the other?"

"You may," Martin said and swatted her. "I love the way your ass blossoms when I spank you."

She lurched forward from the power of the swat and grunted. "Oh, God."

"God has nothing to do with this." Justin pinched her right nipple and added the clip.

The onslaught of feelings, pain, pleasure, joy and tension all overwhelmed her. She dug her toes into the mattress. "Thank you, sirs."

"We've just begun." Martin spanked her again. "What do you want from us?"

"Your love." She shouldn't have said that, but the words tumbled out. "And your hands on my body."

She shivered. A cry came from deep within her as he spanked her again.

Justin pulled an ass plug from his front pocket. "You need this little jewel, too."

She shivered again. "Yes, sir."

Martin spanked her once more, then rounded to face her. "How many?"

"Three, sir." She bit back a groan. "I've been bad and I want another." Her direct demand would grant her more punishment, but she didn't care. "More, sirs."

"Naughty." Martin curled his fingers under her chin and cocked his brow.

She wriggled under his touch. The clips pulled and the bells jingled. As she relaxed, something cool slipped down the crack of her ass. She moaned. The coolness had to be Justin and she welcomed whatever he was going to do. She sighed and backed into him. "More."

Martin tipped his head and met her gaze. "Girl." He brushed his thumb across her bottom lip. "What do you want to do?"

"Please you." She spread her legs farther. When the coolness slid down her ass again, she backed into Justin. "Oh God." The second she did, he pushed something into her rear. The tension and pressure pleased her. She longed for his cock inside her, too.

Martin grinned. "Like that?" He slipped his thumb between her lips.

She sucked greedily, laving her tongue across his digit. She pulled him deep before bobbing her head faster.

"That's beautiful, girl." Martin petted her head. "So pretty sucking on me."

She wanted to answer him, but the words were gone around his thumb. When she backed up, Justin scissored his fingers in her. The added pressure sent her to another level. She moaned. Being used this way, being dominated pleased her. She cried out around Martin's thumb.

"Good girl." Martin grasped her hair and held her on his thumb. "Justin."

She couldn't see what was about to happen, but she could feel it. She sensed the changes and embraced them. When Justin pulled his fingers out, he replaced them with something hard.

She gasped. The fullness overran her mind. She panted and bowed her head, allowing Martin's finger to slip free.

"Now what do you want?" Martin held on to her hair. "My cock in your ass? Or in your pussy?"

"Wherever my masters want." She bowed her head and closed her eyes. "Use me."

"We will." Justin strolled around her and held on to a remote. "Are you sure you want us to use you?" He pressed a button on the fob.

Her ass vibrated and the pulses shot through her body. She splayed her fingers in the bedding and whimpered. "Thank you, sirs." She wasn't sure how to feel. Everything tingled and the clips pulled. She loved the sensations.

"Mine." Martin grasped her hips from behind. Before she could make sense of what was happening, he pushed into her.

The fullness of his cock and the plug in her body made every synapse in her brain misfire. She shuddered as he built into a steady rhythm. Nothing else mattered. The pain on her nipples added to the act.

"I love the way this looks. I want in." Justin remained in front of her, but this time he tipped her head back, forcing her to look into his eyes. He smiled and threaded his fingers into her hair. "Open."

She did as she was told and sucked his cock between her lips. As Martin pushed her forward, she swallowed more of his dick. She simply held on as they rocked her back and forth. She held on as they had their way with her and she loved every second. They'd made her their pleasure being and she couldn't imagine anything else.

Martin reached between her legs and massaged her clit. She shivered and tensed. The orgasm built in her and spiraled to her limbs. Although she cried out around Justin's dick, the sound was muffled.

"Yes, babe." Justin yanked on her hair, holding her tight to his body. "Come with us. Martin's close and I'm not far behind. You're fucking making me crave you. Go over the edge with me."

Martin spanked her. "Fuck me. Go. Come with me."

"With us." Justin let go of her hair, but instead of backing off, he increased his pace. He tipped his head back and growled. When he did, he surged into her mouth and came. Hot seed slid down her throat.

Feeling him come pushed her over the edge. She shivered and her knees buckled. The bells tinged. She swore if Martin wasn't holding her, she'd fall over.

Martin spanked her hard and surged into her. "Fuck. Me." He dug his nails into her bare hips. "Ours."

Not that she wanted to be anywhere else, but right now she had little choice. She whimpered. Her thoughts turned to mush and only Martin and Justin mattered. The rest of the world faded away. Not her pain, frustration or worry. They were gone. Martin and Justin had figured out how to make her feel worthy. Wanted.

Loved.

Now she had to figure out how to make these feelings last. She'd started falling hard for these men and wasn't ready to let them go.

Maybe not ever.

But there wasn't a guarantee they'd feel the same.

She had to risk her heart to get what she wanted.

Could she?

Fuck.

They were worth the risk.

Chapter Twelve

Martin gave himself another moment, then pulled out and swayed. He wasn't sure how she managed to stay in her position. His knees buckled, but he threaded one arm around her and tapped the plug with his free hand. "Breathe, sweetheart."

"I will." She flattened her hands and exhaled. "I'm going to fall over."

"I know you will." He jiggled the plug. "Breathe and relax." He eased the toy from her ass, then tossed the plug onto the bed.

Although he wanted to collapse, he fought through the languidness to scoop her into his arms. He didn't even bother to pull his pants up. Instead, he gathered her to his chest and shuffled around to sit on the bed.

Justin sat beside them and carefully removed the clips. "Breathe, babe. It's okay."

She buried her face against Martin's shoulder. "I'm fine."

"You're more than fine." Martin held her and basked in her closeness.

Justin grinned and arranged her legs on his lap. "You feel wonderful."

Martin agreed a thousand percent. He glanced over at the clock above the door. *Fuck.* They didn't have a lot of time until they had to have her back. They'd promised they'd go with her to the band concert as their second big outing as a triad. Part of him wished they could be together all the time, but the rest of him treasured these moments. Treasured the times he got to be with her. She made him and Justin better. More focused.

"Do you know when we saw you at the club, we were transfixed?" Justin asked and massaged her bare foot. "Couldn't get enough of you."

"He's right." He kissed her forehead. "We wanted to keep you between us. The way you feel is beyond measure. You know how to respond to us and how to make us lose control."

"Do I?" She relaxed in his arms and smiled. "I thought you just saw me as a plaything."

"Oh?" He suppressed a chuckle. "Why would we think that?"

She sat up and a frown marred her brow. "Because I'm not anyone of importance? Because I'm not one of those fancy women you go to dinner with."

"How do you know about who we've had dinner with?" Justin asked. He shook his head. "The last time we went to dinner with a woman was with you at the Skee Ball Shack and before that was when we went with Cindy."

She paled and covered her breasts. "There's another woman?"

"No." Justin sighed, then switched to her other foot. "It's not what you think."

"No?" She tried to scramble off his lap, but Martin held on to her. "Will you listen first? Then you can decide if it's something of importance."

She didn't relax, but also didn't leave him. "Okay."

"Cindy was my wife," Martin said. He wasn't sure he wanted to talk about this part of his life, but she deserved to know. "I thought she was my once-in-a-lifetime girl and I married her, but it turned out that I wasn't really built to have one woman."

Her eyes widened. "So you want another woman." She nodded, then turned her back on him and tried to get up, but he held her fast.

"No." Justin touched her thigh. "Let him speak."

She didn't turn around. The bones in her spine became more pronounced as she leaned over. Martin caressed the curve of her hip. "I love women with a little extra. The curves work for you."

"More cushion for the pushin'?" she asked.

"No. Because it makes you who you are," Martin said. "But you and I need to talk."

"I'm listening."

He gritted his teeth. "Look at me. We're not in a scene right now, but you're not off the hook. I expect you to respect me."

Justin tipped his head once. "I expect the same thing. You might not like what we have to say, but that doesn't mean you get a pass."

She stiffened, then turned to face Martin. "Yes, sirs." Tears shimmered on her lashes, but her cheeks were dry. "I'm listening."

"Better." He snapped his fingers at Justin, who grabbed the robe. When Justin handed him the garment, he draped it around her shoulders. "Now, can you listen?"

"Yes, sirs." She massaged her forehead and sighed. "I'm sorry."

"It's okay." He tucked a lock of her hair behind her ear. "Cindy was my wife, but it wasn't perfect. We were well matched, but she didn't know how to be with me."

"With us," Justin said.

"He's right." Martin grasped her hand. "She loved me, but she couldn't accept that Justin and I are a set. We're not brothers, but we're meant to be a team. She wanted me. We were good together. We had a lot of fun and laughed, but she never wanted Justin around. Just me."

"I don't understand."

"When she married me, I tried to be something I'm not. I'm not meant to love one person. Not meant to be just me and her. Justin's part of it. Part of us," Martin said. "She tried to convince me that she and I were meant to go the distance, but we never were. We had a shelf-life. She would've gotten bored with my life. I'm not the exciting type. I'm not impulsive or thrilling. I'm not even good at going with the flow. That's Justin's job—which is why we're partners."

"What?" She toyed with his shirt. "Martin? I don't understand."

"I married Cindy because I thought I could be a one-woman man and not include my cousin. She didn't want Justin. Couldn't handle living in the same house with him or my working with him. I can't do that. We grew up together, live together and this is our connection. We need someone who can accept that."

"That's it." Justin shrugged. "Pretty cut and dry."

"Have both of you or have neither?" She shifted her gaze between them. "How could she not want you both? You're not at all alike and that's what's fun. You're interesting."

"You'd be surprised." Martin eyed her. "That's how a lot roll."

She picked at the sleeve of the robe. "I suppose they all want your money and what you can provide, too?"

"They do," Justin said.

"And they'll expect you to pay for things?" she asked.

Martin nodded.

"I don't want your money or stuff. It's nice and all, but I don't expect it. I've got a job and savings. I'm not here for you to take care of me." She slid her arm around his neck. "Maybe that's what others desire, but not me."

"I know you're not trying to con us." Martin nuzzled her neck. "But we had to make sure." He'd known from the moment he met her that she wasn't like the others. She could love them both and wasn't interested in the material things. She wasn't afraid to be with him and Justin.

"I want you in our bed and between us every night. Want you here whenever we come home," Justin said. "But that's not realistic yet."

"No." She sighed and caressed Justin's cheek. "I would love to be here all the time, but I can't."

"No, you can't." Martin toyed with a lock of her hair. "You've got responsibilities."

"I do." She exhaled and bowed her head. "One day it'll all get worked out."

"I know." Justin winked. "Be right back."

Martin kissed her temple. "I know this is complicated and a pain in the ass, but we need some time if we want to make it work. We can." He nuzzled her cheek and breathed her in. "You're the one we never thought we'd find. Maybe you're not Cindy, but I don't want another version of her. Don't want that situation. I want someone who is made for us. Who understands and isn't afraid."

"Me?" she whispered.

"You." He remained close to her, nuzzling behind her ear. "I know you've got to get back soon, but I can't wait for every day with you. Every evening. You've brought out the best in us. You taste good, feel wonderful and I want more of everything with you."

"You've got it." She hugged onto him. "I found my heart with you."

"My heart's yours." For as long as she wanted it.

Justin returned to the room. "I should've stayed here."

"Why?" He turned his attention to his cousin. "What happened?"

"Remember the Simons project?" Justin plopped down beside him. "Should've been wrapped up by now."

"But they kept changing their ideas for what they wanted so it got super behind." He remembered all too well. "They can't seem to keep straight the ideas."

"You're right, and they've changed their collective mind again. The blue kitchen isn't good enough. They want green." Justin shook his head. "Anyway, they wanted you to come look at the job and to complain. According to the family, the Hanley brothers haven't done the tile work up to their exacting standards."

He should've guessed. No one could meet those standards. "I need to look right now?"

"This afternoon." Justin pinched the bridge of his nose. "So, we have a job to do."

"We do." He had no desire to end their day together, but he and Justin were the heads of the company so everything came back to them. "Chloe?"

"It's fine with me. This is your job and you need to do it. I can't help that they're possibly asking for something no one can do, but I'm sure you'll figure this all out." She kissed Martin on the lips, then leaned forward and kissed Justin. "Mad and I will be at the concert at seven. If you can make it, then great. If not, then that's okay, too. We understand."

Martin groaned. She was being way too accepting with this. "You're being kind."

"Kind? It's simple understanding," Chloe replied. "If we're a throuple, then this is going to be part of it. Interruptions, misunderstandings, dates, love and all of it. Work can't always be second and I'm fine with that, just like Madelin may need me and I'll have to rush off for that."

"You're pretty damn smart." Martin patted her thigh. "And yes, I do have to get this handled."

"So handle it." She grinned and rested her forehead on his. "I'm not going anywhere. I mean...I'm going home, but I'm still yours. Both of yours."

"I never doubted you." Justin kissed her cheek. "Want me to give you a ride home?"

"Probably should." She left Martin's lap. "I didn't bring anything to dress in, but I should use the powder room."

"We'll sort something out for your clothes." Martin stood and sighed. "You can wear that robe as a wrap dress. With your jacket over top, no one will be the wiser."

"Thank you." She grinned and the color returned to her cheeks.

"I'll show you to the bathroom," Justin said. "This way." He left the room with Chloe right behind him.

Martin growled, then stuffed himself back in his trousers. *Jesus H. Christ.* Clients would be the death of him. He picked up the toy and the clips, then put the toy in the hidden sink and the clips on the counter. Before he went to the Simons house, he needed to speak to Jack Hanley. If anyone knew what was going on, it'd be him. He grabbed Justin's phone, then swiped to Jack's number.

After three rings, Jack answered. "I thought I'd hear from you."

"You have. I want your side of this. Justin spoke to Simons, so I have their side." He leaned against the counter and crossed his ankles. "What's going on?"

"Plain and simple, the tile work is fine. It's right up to our standards, but it's blue and they want green. Or green and they want blue. We've changed it out twice, with one being at our expense. No matter what we do, it's not right. Mr. Simons already told us he could do it better and I have half a mind to let him."

"He'll probably do it anyway." He knew Mr. Simons. The man thought everything he'd done was better than the professionals, but his skills weren't always as honed as he believed. "What do you suggest?"

"You look at the project and make your judgment. I trust you and I have the feeling you'll see it the way I do—that it's a foolish notion to keep changing the damn tiles. It's ruining the wall and wasting a lot of time."

"That and money." He noticed his cousin returning to the room. "We'll visit the job site today and see what's going on. Are you there?"

"We are, and will be until six."

"Fine." He nodded to his cousin. "Shouldn't be more than an hour."

"Sounds good." Jack hung up.

Martin handed the phone to Justin. "This is a shit show."

"It is, but this is why we're the bosses. We can make decisions on what to do." Justin widened his stance and placed his hands on his hips. "I don't want to let her down, but we've got to sort this out. Besides, I'd love a good concert."

"It's a high school band competition." But he agreed with Justin. "Is she ready?"

"She will be. Are you?" Justin asked.

"I need to grab my jacket." He preferred to dress in business casual for trips to job sites. "I'll meet you in the kitchen in five minutes."

"You've got it." Justin clapped him on the shoulder, then left the room.

He followed close on his cousin's heels, then raced up the stairs to his bedroom. He grabbed the first sport coat he could find, then hurried back to the ground floor.

Chloe stood with Justin in the kitchen. "Look at you," she said. "Dapper."

"I'm trying to." He straightened the coat. "We've got to speak to some of the workers and I prefer to visit the sites dressed like I have some authority."

"I'll get mine." Justin disappeared, leaving her alone with Martin.

"I'm sorry we had to interrupt the scene." He grasped her hand. "And we may be late to the concert."

"I don't mind." She tucked against him. "Things happen."

"They do."

"I did a lot of thinking while we were both indisposed. I'm thinking like a child, expecting you both to pay limitless attention to me. It's not possible. We're all adults and things come up. Big deal. You've given me so much — more than I deserve. You see me as something other than a waste. I'm not that chubby girl or the extra friend. When you and Justin look at me, I feel desired. Special. I feel like I'm the only woman in the room."

"You might as well be. You're our curvy, beautiful dream girl who's stepped out of our fantasies and into our life. We're not letting you go." He kissed her, needing to taste every last bit of Chloe. He sucked on her tongue, then slipped his arm around her. He patted her ass. When she curled tighter into him, she parted her legs and rode his thigh. Her neediness would wear him down. She'd make him change everything in his life willingly for her. She was the one.

"I see how it feels to walk in on something and I can't say I like it, but I do like the view. Fuck," Justin said. "It's hot."

Martin broke the kiss, but kept her in his arms. He said nothing and shook his head. He'd bet it was hot to see them together. Just as hot as it was to see her giving herself over to Justin.

Her breath tickled Martin's cheek. "Guess we got caught."

"Nah." Martin patted her ass again. "Is the car ready?"

Justin nodded. "When you are."

"We should go." She held on to Martin, but grasped Justin's hand with her free one. "Soon, everything will be the way it should be and we won't have to worry about these kinds of interruptions. Besides, I need to get home. She'll be there in an hour and I don't want her to catch me in this."

"You look fantastic," Justin said. "But I get it."

"I do, too." Martin walked with her to the door. "Let's go. I don't want to do this, but we need to get it done before we can have fun."

"You're right." She kissed him on the cheek. "But can we take the truck? That way we can all sit together?"

Martin laughed and his mind eased. The tension of the impending meeting evaporated with her simple request. "That's the best thing I've heard in a while. Maybe ever." He could sit on one side and Justin on the other. Both could fondle her while they rode and everyone would be happy. They'd get to touch her and she'd get off.

What a great way to race across town.

He couldn't wait to get the meeting finished so he could return to their girl and get her off in the best, sexiest way possible—between them.

Chapter Thirteen

Chloe allowed them to take her home and basked in the thrill of being between them. Justin and Martin knew how to make a simple ride the most erotic thing she'd ever experienced. As Justin drove, he rested his hand on her thigh. Martin parted her coat over the robe to toy with her sensitive pussy. Each time he touched her, she nearly screamed with pleasure. He slipped a finger into her cunt, pushing in and caressing her. He nudged her to the edge. The climaxes were coming faster and easier now. Like he knew how to play her body.

When Justin stopped in front of her apartment, she panted and willed her legs to cooperate. Fuck. She'd have to not only walk up to the front door, but unlock it and duck inside all on her own.

She'd have to shower and get herself ready for the concert as well as presentable for her niece.

Not impossible, but it wouldn't be easy.

"We'll see you in a few hours, tops," Justin said. He kissed her, nipping on her tongue. "Don't forget me."

"We couldn't." She allowed Martin to turn her head. He withdrew his fingers, then traced his finger across her lips. "Martin."

"Good?" His eyes flashed.

"Very good." She sucked greedily on his finger, licking him clean. "I'll look for both of you."

"You'd better." Martin exited the truck before her, then helped her out of the vehicle. He stayed next to the door as she wobbled to her apartment.

When she looked back, he and Justin were still where she'd left them in the lot. She managed to unlock the door. Once inside, she waved. Martin climbed back into the truck before Justin pulled away. She sagged against the sofa. She'd made it home before Madelin. *Good.*

Chloe rushed into her bedroom. She selected clothes for the concert, then carried the bundle to the bathroom. Her ass stung from the spankings and her skin was on fire in a good way. She hadn't felt this alive in so long. She turned on the water and waited for the steam to billow before she stripped. The heat of the water surrounded her as she stepped into the stall. The spray bit into her skin. She ducked her head under the showerhead. Thoughts flew through her mind. Memories of being with Justin and Martin. The excitement of being used. The way their hands felt on her body. The fullness. The passion. Her nipples ached under the water and she turned her back on the spray as she washed her hair.

She hadn't done anything wrong, being with them. It wasn't wrong to love two men.

She paused and her breath wrenched in her throat. Love. Yeah, that's what she felt. Down to her core and washed under with no desire to surface. She cared about them. Sure, this was fast. Good God. She wasn't sure how old they were. But she'd fallen hard for them.

Although the situation wasn't wrong, she had to switch gears.

She couldn't be in love with them. Sure, they said the right things and treated her with dignity, but she wasn't like Darinda. She wasn't classy or elegant. She didn't have poise or know what fork to use when at a formal setting.

Besides, she was working class. They needed someone high-powered like them.

She finished washing her hair, then added conditioner before rinsing that, too. Why did the sexy guys have to be complicated? Why couldn't she accept the gift they were giving her? They were practically begging her to be with them.

But she was afraid.

Afraid they'd change their mind. That they'd see she wasn't fancy or cultured. They'd want someone younger. Prettier. Someone better than her.

"Aunt Chloe?"

She snapped out of her pity party and finished her shower, then turned off the water. "Mad?"

"I'm home." Madelin knocked on the door. "I don't have homework. Got it done in study hall. Shocked the hell out of my teacher when I stopped after the bell to ask questions."

She dried off and dressed in no time, then opened the door. "You're a smart kid. I'm not surprised you got it done. What was the question?"

"It's about family trees." Mad popped the lid on a container of peanut butter bites. "I told her mine's complicated and she laughed. Can you believe it? The teacher laughed."

"Was it nervous?"

"Probably."

She brushed her hair out as the steam cleared. "And when you explained it?"

"She said to do the best I could. I bet she calls Mom tonight." Madelin ate a couple of the bites. "I'm going to get my ass handed to me."

"First, language." She put the brush down, then collected her pile of clothing. "Second, if they do call your mother, then they do."

"Mom will be angry."

"About what?" She carried the clothes to her bedroom. "Unless you said you don't have a mother or something out of left field like that, then there shouldn't be an issue."

"I told the teacher that my mother is being unreasonable and I live with my aunt." Madelin sat on the bed. "I also talked to her about the situation with Sam."

"And?" She sat beside her niece. "What'd she say?"

"Sam pulled that prank on two other girls, which tells me he wasn't interested in me. That's okay. I don't like him that way, so it's fine."

"That's good, isn't it?"

"It is." Madelin put the container down. "I don't dislike him, but I don't like him that way."

"Is there someone else?"

"Kind of." She shrugged. "I like a guy named Key. He's a year older and plays trombone. I wanted to introduce you to him tonight."

"Oh?" She appreciated the level of trust between them. "So? Tell me about him." She applied her makeup as her niece spoke.

"He's tall, skinny and a nerd, but like a fifties rock star nerdy. He's wicked good at music and hella smart. He's in algebra two already and speaks geometry because he managed to explain what we're doing in geometry enough that I understand it. I don't math well." Madelin put the lid on the container. "He's not popular, but not an outcast. He's got deep brown eyes and a goofy smile."

"He does, does he?" She put the mascara down. "The goofy smile on your face tells me there's a little more here than just innocence. You're going to tell me he's your boyfriend, aren't you?"

Her eyes widened and she paled, then covered her face with both hands. "You weren't supposed to pick that up so fast!"

"I'm not clueless. I do know what it's like to fall for someone and to try to hide that you like them. I'm guessing it's almost impossible to hide that smile?" She put her makeup away. "You have a concert tonight. Aren't you supposed to be getting around for it? We need to get there in about forty-five minutes, don't we?"

"We do." Madelin didn't move. "I'm worried Mom will show up and freak out."

"If she does, then we'll deal with it. You focus on your music and doing your best. The band needs you to be on your game." She left her makeup table and joined Madelin on the bed. "Your mom cares, but she's struggling. I don't know why, but she is. She's not mad at you, I promise. She's angry with herself for being confused and in so deep. But that's her problem, not yours. You focus on you and keep moving forward."

Madelin stared at her. "Why are you so calm about this? I'm scared."

"Because I know your mother. I don't know why she's gotten herself this twisted up, but she'll figure it out, okay?"

"Okay."

"Are you supposed to wear the dress uniforms?"

"No, it's casual because it's the Fall Fling Concert. Everyone is wearing their summer ones." Madelin left the bed and picked up the container. "Mine's clean, but I need to change."

"Okay."

Madelin paused in the doorway. "Are Martin and Justin going to be there?"

"They are. Don't you want them to be?" She stood and smoothed her blouse. "Don't you like them?"

"No." Madelin put both hands up. "I like them a lot and I'm pretty sure they like you. They're good for you. You're not as stressed like you used to be. It's nice."

"Stabilizing?"

"Yes."

"Then that's a good thing. You need some stable in your life," she said. "How's Kindra?"

"She's dating Evan now. I swear she switches guys like her shoes, but they don't seem to care." Madelin shrugged, then left the doorway. "I don't understand her, but we don't talk about boys."

"Are you still talking?"

"I just texted her when I got home." Madelin disappeared into the other bedroom.

She opted to head to the kitchen and rifled through the cabinets in search of something for supper. "Mad?

Are they serving food at this?" She hadn't been given any information on donating food or drinks to the cause tonight.

"Yes." Madelin walked into the kitchen. She'd changed her shirt and her hair stuck out at odd angles. "The boosters donated it, so we don't have to eat before."

"Okay." That helped because the cupboards were bare. "I've got some cash on me. Why don't we finish getting around and head out so you're not late?"

"I need to change my jeans, but then we can go. I've got my flute by the door." Madelin disappeared again.

She snorted to herself and shook her head. For not being a mother or even considered becoming one, she'd picked up the rhythm with Madelin. Things weren't perfect, but they weren't bad, either. She gathered her phone, purse and keys, then stepped into her mules before waiting at the door for Madelin.

Madelin rushed around the corner and grabbed her flute case from the chair. "I'm ready."

"Then let's go." She followed her niece out of the apartment and locked up behind them, then strode to the car. Once behind the wheel, she engaged the engine before backing out of her spot. She drove across town, expecting her phone to ring at any moment with an angry call from her sister.

She reached the school a few minutes later and dropped Madelin off at the band room door. "I'll meet you in the audience after and you'd better believe I'll be taking photos."

"Thanks, Auntie Chloe." Madelin hesitated a moment, then hugged Chloe before leaving the car.

Chloe waited for Madelin to disappear into the building before selecting a parking spot over by the gymnasium. When she left the car, she spotted Martin and Justin.

"You're here." She slammed her door and locked the car. "I didn't expect you to make it."

"We're miracle workers." Justin embraced her first. "And the problem wasn't as big as we thought."

"No?" She linked arms with him, then with Martin. "How'd you figure that out?"

"We visited the job site and talked to the owners. The tile work was fine, but they hadn't settled on a color and thought they could keep switching it out as they pleased. They can if they pay for it, but it does damage the wall. So…we convinced them that the color currently on the wall is high end, unique and they're the only ones in the Northern United States to have it, so that helped. I think it's diffused enough for now," Martin said. "But we also promised you we'd be here, so we're here."

"You did." She walked with them to the gym doors. "It's a couple bucks to get in and there's a concession stand, I'm told." She let go and opened her purse.

"Babe, we've got this. Our treat." Justin surged forward and paid for the threesome to enter the concert.

"You don't have to," she muttered.

"Why not?" Martin picked up a program. "You're our girl."

"I know, but…" She tensed. "It's still something I'm wrapping my mind around."

"We know." Justin directed her to the line for the concession stand. "You don't have to overthink this."

"No?" She waited in line with them. "I'm scared."

"About what?" Martin steered her away from the line to a quieter area in the lobby. "You don't have to be afraid of us."

"I'm scared you'll realize I'm a stand-in mom and that I'm twenty-eight, not twenty-one. That I'm not classy and I like the games we play. I'm not the poster child for girlfriend material for men like you." There. She'd said it.

"Men like us?"

"Yeah." She glanced about in case her sister came rushing up to her. She hadn't seen Melinda yet, but that didn't mean much. "You're men of means. You know people. You do things."

"And you?" Martin tipped his head. "What about you?"

"I'm boring. I club, sure, but I can't do that all the time. I have to take care of Mad until my sister sorts her life out. That's not exciting or elegant." It was boring and mom-ish. Certainly not the kind of woman who'd get involved in threesomes. But she loved being with them both.

"Who says you're boring? I don't. Justin doesn't. We think you're fantastic the way you are." Martin curled his fingers under her chin. "There's something to be said for being the right woman. You might not be the younger model, but we don't want that. Might not be those other things you think you're not, but that doesn't matter. We're not interested in what you're not. We're interested in who you are. The one who makes us laugh. Who doesn't shrink away from our responsibilities at work. Who is adorable and sweet and fits between us. That's you."

She wanted to argue, but why?

"If I wanted someone else, I'd find them, but I don't. Justin agrees." He brushed his nose along hers. "You matter to us. Madelin does, too. We love seeing you blossom with her."

"You noticed?"

"We did." Martin's eyes flashed. "And besides, tonight is for her. Let's make her feel special. Yeah?"

"Let's." She held Martin's hand as Justin approached. He balanced a box with three bottles of water, three hotdogs and two bags of chips. "Want some help?" she asked and accepted the box. "You got a lot."

"I bought some candy, too. It helps the band fund." Justin grinned. "And why not help? I dumped a ten into the donation can, too."

"You're a gem." She kissed him on the cheek. "I'm sure the band appreciates it."

"Why not help?" Justin nodded to the tables. "The concert doesn't start for another twenty minutes. We've got time to eat before finding a place to park it."

"What a way with words." Martin rolled his eyes. "But he's got a point. I'm hungry."

"They had corndogs, too, but I wasn't sure if you'd want one." Justin placed the bottles on the table. He frowned and fiddled with the lid of the closest bottle. "Do you know a woman with blond hair?"

"Me?" She glanced over at Martin. "Or him?"

Martin snorted. "Fuck me. That's Cindy's sister."

Justin sank onto the bench. "Fuck."

"I'll be right back." Martin left the table and ducked into the crowd.

"Is that a bad thing?" Besides the fact that her stomach churned didn't matter. She kept her focus on Justin. "Will it be tense?"

"I don't know. After Cindy died, he didn't have much to do with her family. They blame him for the accident, even though he wasn't even there. He hadn't upset Cindy and it was truly an accident, but that didn't matter. She died and he didn't, and they wanted a pound of flesh."

"Umm… I'm speechless." She opened the foil on her hotdog. "You got mustard and onions."

"I did. Was that wrong?" Justin opened the second bottle. "Sorry."

"It's not wrong, if you don't want to kiss me later. I'll stink of onions." She laughed to try to break the tension. "But I suppose if you got them all with onions, we'll be gross together."

"We will." He laughed and shook his head. "I didn't consider it'd be smelly when I dressed the dogs. Just tried to hurry."

"It's fine." She winked, then bit into her hotdog. "They grilled them, not boiled. Nice."

"They've got a couple funny little tabletop indoor grills over there. It's quite a system." Justin ate half of his hotdog, then drank the water.

"Think they're arguing, or okay?" she asked.

"I don't know, but there's a woman coming our direction and she seems pissed. What is it with finding angry people today? I don't know who she is, but she's right behind you." Justin nodded. "Your sister?"

"Fuck me," she murmured.

"Later." He winked, then stood. "Hello."

She sighed and turned, knowing her sister had to be behind her. Sure enough, Melinda clutched her purse and stared at Chloe.

"I see you're here." Melinda nodded. "You made it."

She balled the foil from her hotdog and shifted to face her sister. "Have a seat." She gestured to the bench. "Please?"

Melinda sank onto the seat and huffed. "I suppose you're allowing her to do whatever she wants."

"Okay, first. This is Justin, my boyfriend. Justin, this is my sister, Melinda." She exhaled to buy a second to think. "As for what Mad is doing, she's not running wild. In fact, she's getting her homework done, her grades are up and she's happy. She's even got a young man she's interested in. He seems nice and suits her well. I've seen her flourish and it's not because she's with me. It's because she's being herself."

Melinda narrowed her eyes, then turned her attention to Justin. "So you're the boyfriend?"

"Chloe's, yes, not Madelin's." Justin offered his hand. When she didn't bother to shake hands, he withdrew. "You're the sister. It's nice to meet you."

"I'm sure you've heard a lot about me. Probably that I'm a bad person and terrible. I'm mean to my daughter?" Melinda straightened her blouse. "Or maybe that I'm struggling with my relationships."

"Okay." Chloe shot up from her seat. "The concert starts in about ten minutes. Why don't you get us some seats and I'll talk to my sister? Yes?"

Justin collected the remainder of the food and nodded. "You bet. I'll let Martin know where we're at and we'll find you."

"Thanks." She paused. "Will you take pictures if we don't make it in right away? I promised Mad I'd take pictures."

"Sure will." He kissed her cheek, then nodded to Melinda. "See you in a little bit."

She threaded her arm around Melinda's and dragged her out to the parking lot. Once they were away from too many prying ears, she let go. "Okay, so let's get this out."

"What do you mean? We're late for the concert." Melinda tried to dart into the building, but Chloe stood in her way.

"Stop." Chloe grasped Melinda's arms. "Stop."

"You're taking my daughter," Melinda snapped. She lowered her voice. "You're making me look bad. You've got a boyfriend, you're happy and adjusted and my daughter is now happy and adjusted. I'm a fucking mess and you're succeeding. It's not right."

"Because you're supposed to be the successful one and I'm supposed to be the hot mess?" She let go and backed up a step. "That's what this is all about?"

"Maybe."

"You're married to one man, fucking another and you're worried your daughter will see it? Trust me. She's seen and she's upset. Then there's your boyfriend you're fucking who is treating your daughter like shit. Did you know that?" Chloe asked. She kept her voice even. "Is he abusing her? I should've reported it. Damn it."

"He's not."

"Don't argue with me on this one. I finally got her to open up to me. It's her story to tell, but if even a shred of what she's saying is true, then Earl needs to be removed from the home," Chloe said. "I'm serious, and if David finds out, he'll be pissed. He will make sure she's taken from you."

Melinda opened her mouth but didn't speak.

"I'm guessing from your silence, it's probably true." Chloe hooked her fingers in her front pockets. "You don't love David any longer. I get it. People change their mind and hearts grow cold, but that doesn't mean you screw around on them. David deserves better."

Melinda bowed her head. "I know."

"Then why are you doing that to him?" she asked her sister. "My God. David isn't perfect and he's not home much, but he's trying. Earl is a mess."

"He is." Melinda sighed and picked at her sleeve. "Earl's abusing me, too, but I can't seem to get loose. I can't tell David because it'll kill him, but I made a mistake when I hooked up with Earl. That's why I'm not begging her to come home. I know it's a shit show."

"What?" she whispered. She hadn't expected her sister to say any of these things. "I didn't know."

"I've been struggling for a while. I spiraled out of control because of David being gone. I didn't know how to handle him always being on the road and I thought that if I hooked up with Earl, then things would be okay, but they weren't. I miss David, but I don't know how to ask him to come home. He knows things are fucked up and he won't talk to me." Melinda grasped Chloe's arms. "I told myself it was because you're supposed to be the mess, but the truth is I've always been a mess. I've had everything handed to me and haven't had to work for much. Now that I've got to sort through this shit, I can't. I'm not ready. But you? You're sailing and it's irritating because I can't seem to make this work. That's why I let her stay with you. I encouraged her. I knew he was hurting her and verbally abusing her, so I got her out. I can't yet, but I could help her."

"Mel..." She should've guessed this was bigger and more complicated than she'd originally thought.

"Just let me watch her from afar and I'll figure out how to fix this. I'll get my kid back and I'll get rid of my fuck friend. I'll get my husband back, too. We deserve better and you're more than we should have." Melinda trembled. "I just...I fucked this all up."

"Okay." She held on to her sister. "Things are out of sorts and you should leave his ass right now, but you've got to do what you need when you need to. I'm here for you. I'm here for Mad. I don't know how to fix this, but you do and you will."

"I will."

She hugged her sister, feeling like she'd made no progress, but she understood the situation better. "Go watch her. She's proud of what she's done and her boyfriend is a lanky trombone player. She's a good kid with a good head on her shoulders. She's going to be okay and I'll make sure she stays that way. I've got you both."

"Thanks." Melinda let go and darted into the building.

When she turned, Chloe ran headlong into Martin. "Sorry."

"You okay?" He rubbed her back. "You look spooked."

"It's a long story, but my niece is with me for a damn good reason and I won't let her down." She bumped shoulders with Martin. "I know this isn't what you expected for us, but there's a reason."

"I know there is." He kissed her temple. "Justin told me where he's sitting, so we'll find him. We'll take photos of Mad and you can talk to us about this later. I don't know what's going on, but I'm here and I'm not quitting on you. Neither is Justin. Understand me?"

She did. She hugged him tight and waited a beat before going into the building. "Thank you."

"I told you. We've got you no matter what." Martin walked with her to the gym. The music hadn't started yet, but the first band had marched into place.

Chloe didn't see her sister, but she spotted Madelin. She waved, then pulled her phone from her pocket and took photos. Things weren't perfect and she'd have to do a lot of explaining, but right now, the one thing that mattered was getting attention. She'd do whatever she had to for Madelin to know she was loved.

With Martin and Justin at her side, she'd make this work. For Madelin and for herself. She had no other choice. Her niece needed a better chance in life. Beyond that, Chloe had to do this for herself. She'd fallen in love with her men.

She wasn't losing this chance at love.

No way.

Chapter Fourteen

Justin walked out of the gym after the concert swearing he'd go deaf, but he regretted nothing. The bands had been better than he'd expected and he'd forgotten how much he enjoyed live music. Besides, he'd spent the evening with his cousin and their girl. Who could want more than that?

Not him.

He stood among the crowd and waited for Chloe to take photos with her niece. Martin strode up to him.

"That was something." Martin shoved his hands into his pockets. "I don't remember it being that...I don't know."

"Loud?"

"Yeah." Martin nodded. "We never had this much pep when we were in school."

"You and I weren't interested in being in school. You couldn't wait to get to college and I just wanted to survive high school." He'd hated the environment of the time because he was a creative and athletic, but not particularly popular. He couldn't live up to Martin's legacy at school. Martin had been a runner, smart and got along well with everyone. Justin had been class treasurer.

"You did hate it." Martin shook his head. "I see them coming. Did you see her sister showed up?"

"I did." He'd tried to ignore what was said and not push Chloe to talk. "Eventually, she'll tell us what went on."

"She will."

"We need to tell her that we did a little too much research on her and take the repercussions of it," Justin said. "She might not like that we did so much orchestration."

"We started to tell her."

"Maybe, but we didn't tell her we essentially blocked anyone else from talking to her that night at the club. Once we caught sight of her, we pounced. What if she doesn't like that? She might not."

"I don't." Chloe folded her arms and glared at them. "You said you'd orchestrated plenty for me, but you really pushed people away? You pulled every string."

"I…" Martin's shoulders sagged. "Wait."

"You can't control everything. I don't want to be controlled that way." Chloe held up both hands. "I need some space. Today was fantastic and I'd love to do it again, but not right now. Not any time soon. Leave me alone."

"Wait." Justin touched her arm, careful not to grab her. "It's not like that. Please."

"Just…" She backed away from him.

"What made you change your mind? We were good," Martin said. "What caused this?"

"You're talking about me like I don't exist and I don't like that kind of control. I thought I could handle it, but I need to be my own person outside of certain circumstances. You want someone you can order around and I'm not her." Chloe turned on her heel and walked away.

"That just happened, didn't I?" Justin snorted. "I don't know what it was, but it happened."

"We screwed up."

"We did." His stomach churned. "We pushed a little too hard and treated her like a business deal. Like something we could control, but she's not that person. She shouldn't be. We should have her on a pedestal and give her the love and devotion she wants. She deserves."

"You're right." Martin groaned. "But this is yet another time she's walked away from us."

"And we pushed too hard, but I don't think this is all on us. Something tells me there's more going on here."

"There has to be." Martin groaned. "Are you fucking kidding me? This night can't get any worse."

"What?"

"First, Cindy's half-sister is here with her daughter, who's in the Cardinal band. She saw me and threw a fit because she doesn't think I should be anywhere near her. I'm not." Martin growled. "Fuck me. You know?"

"I do." The past with Cindy had been more complicated than anyone knew and Martin shouldn't have to keep paying for it.

"Your past is about to slap you, so watch out." Martin groaned and walked away.

His past? What? He still wasn't sure what Martin was upset about, but when he glanced over his shoulder, he noticed the reason. Aline strode up to him.

He hadn't thought about Aline in so long. Like, since the month they'd been together. She'd been fun when they'd been a couple in their twenties, but wouldn't have worked in the long-term because he hadn't wanted to settle down back then.

"So that is you." Aline swept her gaze over him. "You're at a high school band concert? Mr. High-Powered-I'll-Kick-Your-Ass is here? Who'd you knock up? The kid is a surprise kid? Or you knew and kept it hidden?"

"None of the above." He wasn't about to back down because he hadn't done anything wrong. "You're here."

"I am."

"Which band?"

"My son's in the Ranger band." She narrowed her eyes.

"Cool." He hadn't been looking at the various bands to see if any of them resembled him. "Are you okay?"

"You're that cold, aren't you?"

"I'm not, but quite frankly, you marched up to me like you're pissed and you've got a bone to pick with me, so excuse me for being on my guard." He hooked his fingers in his front pockets and kept his frustration in check. "What can I do for you?"

"Lots of things. I saw you're here with someone. She's cute, but does she know you and Martin are together?"

"She does and she was here with both of us."

She cocked her brow, then regained her composure. "She knows about what you two do?"

"She knows everything and she's fine with it, which is all you need to know." He lowered his voice. "It's not everyone's information to know, but you do."

"I do." She narrowed her eyes and chewed on the corner of her mouth. "I see."

"I'm glad. Now, what can I do for you?" he asked. "You came over here on a mission, so what is it?"

She stared at him a moment, then rested her hands on her hips. "You and I split but you never said why. You're here and I didn't think you'd settle down. What gives? What's different with her than with me?"

"It's not so much that she's different, but I'm different," he said. "I grew up. You and I got together when I was in my twenties and full of myself. I didn't want to be tied down and I acted like it. It wasn't cool or kind. I took what I wanted and didn't care who I hurt—including you. I hit thirty-eight and realized my life was going by without much to show for it. Why are you looking for closure now?"

"I deserve it," she said. "So you grew up?"

"I matured, yeah. I've got the business and that's fine. We've got money, but what do we have to show for it?"

"You've got more money than God," she snapped.

"It's more than that." She'd never understand. "I wanted more from my life. Money is fine, but if you don't have anyone to share it with, then it's pointless. So we went looking for someone who could handle us. Who wanted us, not the money."

"You don't think that was me?"

"I don't know." He hadn't given them a chance to find out. "But it doesn't matter. You're happy now. You've got a son and a relationship. You've got it all."

"Who says I do?" She cocked her hip. "I could always use a few bucks. He's growing out of clothes faster than I can keep up and don't ask me about his shoes."

Ah, so she wants money. "I see."

"You'll find out. She's got a kid? Boy or girl?"

"Girl." He clipped the word. "So?"

"Then you've got makeup and clothes and shoes and all the other stuff. You'll be bled dry." She patted his chest. "If you ever want to part with some of that cash, then you tell me. I can use it and you've got too much."

"Do I?"

"You do and should share, but you'll know what to do with it." She tugged him close and kissed him. "Oh, and she's watching. I hope this makes her hurt in the way you made me hurt when you walked away. You can all fuck off."

"You have a nice day, too." He caught sight of Chloe at the door. Sure enough, she'd seen Aline kiss him. She didn't know what had happened, but she'd seen it and that'd fucked him over.

Aline smiled before she walked away.

Justin strode toward Chloe, but she darted out of the way before he could get close. Martin waited at the door and grabbed Justin's arm. "I know," Martin said. "I saw. You were set up."

"I was." He sighed. "And we're fucked."

"Not entirely." Martin snapped his fingers and nodded in the direction of the truck. "We'll get this sorted out, but you and I have to make a plan. We can't just send flowers or a sweet box of chocolates."

"No, we can't." He wasn't sure what to do. A dull ache started behind his eyes and he wanted to go home. "Let's get out of here."

"I'll drive."

He followed Martin to the truck. "Why does love have to be complicated?"

"Love?" Martin stopped short. "Did you just say what I think you did?"

"I did." He left Martin behind and jogged up to the truck. Without another word, he climbed onto the passenger seat. He'd said what he'd meant and regretted nothing.

Martin joined him in the truck. He slammed the door, but didn't engage the engine. "Love?"

"Yes." He stared straight ahead. "I love her."

"I see."

"You don't?"

"No one said that." Martin stuffed the key into the ignition and turned the truck on. He drove out of the lot, putting space between them and the school. "I hadn't thought about whether I'm in love or not. I've simply been riding the wave."

"I bet you are." He was, too. He'd never felt this way about anyone before and the notion scared him. She was one of the few people he didn't want to lose. He couldn't see his life without her. This wasn't the usual for him. He tended to love and leave, but the more time he spent with her and with her between him and Martin, the more he liked it. He couldn't see his life without her.

"What changed your mind? You told me you were a bachelor for life." Martin drove out to the edge of town. "Talk to me."

"Getting older changed me." He picked at the stitching on the door upholstery. "I realized I was pushing everyone who mattered away from me and I wasn't pulling anyone in close. The more I kept people out, other than you, the more I'd protect myself. I didn't want to end up like my fucking father."

God damn it. He hadn't wanted to bring that up. Never wanted to think about it again. His father hadn't been the patriarch he should've been. He'd tried to bury the pain of his upbringing, but apparently the past didn't want to be buried.

"Justin?" Martin pulled off at the park on the edge of town and stopped in the empty lot. "It's okay."

"No. It's not." He unbuckled his belt and left the truck. He strode halfway around the pond to the far side. The fury he'd held on to for years finally came loose. He couldn't hear Martin coming up behind him, but he felt him. "That fucker didn't know how to be a dad. All he knew how to do was fuck around and leave. He'd come into the family situation and make comments, then leave. He'd beat the shit out of me because I wasn't what he wanted. He'd punish me for being creative. Punish me for being quiet. He's the reason I didn't talk about my past. He's the reason I leave before I get in too deep. Don't get hurt. If I don't get hurt, then I'm fine. It's fucked."

Martin rested his hand on Justin's shoulder. He didn't say anything, but instead squeezed.

"I swore I wouldn't do anything to anyone that he'd done to me." He bowed his head. "Fucker."

"You're not him," Martin murmured. "You're eons from him."

"Am I?" He stared out at the landscape. "Fuck me. I'm just as bad."

"No." Martin let go and stepped in front of him. "You're not at all. Look at me."

He couldn't.

"I wasn't there the entire time you were growing up, but I knew there was a problem. I knew something changed when you'd withdrawn in high school. I didn't want to push you to talk, but I've been waiting on this day." Martin grasped him by the shoulders, then hugged him. "He had no right to hurt you, but you're not him. You never will be. You've got something he never did—heart. Heart and tenderness. That's what I see. That's what Chloe sees."

"Chloe?" He groaned and shrugged away from his cousin. "I fucked it up with her, too."

"Because she saw you get a kiss from Aline?"

"Yes." How did Martin not understand this?

"She's upset right now, but this isn't nearly as bad as it looks. All you have to do is explain. I know she'll listen to you." Martin's shoulders sagged. "This isn't like other situations. You're right. She's the one and I'm in love with her, too. She's that piece I've been looking for. The one we can share and love and have forever."

Martin made sense, but he wasn't sure how to fix this problem. They couldn't throw money at it. Couldn't throw their weight around, either. He rested his hands on his hips and bowed his head. Tears streamed down his cheeks and he thanked God the only person who could see him was Martin. He refused to be this bare in front of anyone else. "Fuck," he muttered.

"I get it. This is complicated and messy and fucked up, but you had to get that out," Martin said. "You had to be yourself and the only way you can do that is to let go of what he did. He's a monster and never deserved to have kids. He got lucky as hell to have you as his son and he fucked up the chance. The one thing he did right was to show you how not to be a man—how not to be like him and you've done that. You're not one iota like him."

"No?" He finally looked at his cousin. "I feel exactly like him."

"You're not."

"Why did he do that to me? Why did he treat me like shit?" The anger he'd been holding on to deflated and he threw himself into his cousin's arms to sob. Fuck, he hated crying.

"I don't know why he did that other than he's a bully and a bastard. He didn't have to do it or have the right to, but you're better for it. You're finding your way and you've got your footing. Now it's time to show the woman we both love that we're ready for this chance. This commitment. We can do it."

He dried his face and tried to regain his composure. Fuck, this was hard. He'd never wanted to talk about his father or his past and he knew Martin had some idea of what'd happened. Martin had been there. He might not have known every detail, but Martin was aware.

"It's okay to break down. Hell, if you hadn't finally, you'd have exploded." Martin stepped away from him, giving him space. "My God. You've had that tucked down for a long time. I'm surprised you held on to it all these years. It's okay."

"I know." He exhaled and scrubbed the back of his hand across his face. "I thought if I buried it, then I could tell myself it hadn't happened and if I lied to myself that it hadn't happened, I could pretend I'd made it all up."

"That's fucked up."

"It is." And it was time to let go. He cleared his throat and rifled his fingers through his hair. "So, what do we do? I seem to have messed a lot up, but it's not beyond fixing."

"Never is." Martin nodded to the truck. "Let's go back to the house and have a think on it. By the time tomorrow rolls around, we'll have a plan."

"We will." He followed his cousin to the truck and collapsed on the seat. Allowing himself to let go of his past had worn him out. His knees buckled. Good thing the seat was right there. He managed to shut the door and buckle up before Martin drove off.

Things were in disarray with Chloe, but he and Martin were on the same page. They'd figure out how to win her back and make her theirs for the duration. They wanted her silly, smart, goofy…her everything. She made his heart beat and he knew she did the same for Martin.

Soon, they'd have what they all wanted and they'd be happy.

Until then, he'd live with figuring it all out.

Chapter Fifteen

Chloe spent the next two days thinking about what she'd done with Martin and Justin, but also what she'd seen. She'd given her body to them and they had her heart, despite her best efforts to keep it protected. What did she have to show for it?

Justin kissing someone else.

Martin being married before.

She was replaceable and they could replace her at any moment.

She touched the collar. She hadn't tried to remove the piece of jewelry, but she wondered if it was even worth having on. If they didn't want to keep her, she shouldn't be wearing the collar.

"Auntie Chloe?" Madelin strolled into the kitchen. "Are you okay?"

"I'm fine." She flattened her hands on the counter and forced a smile. "Why do you ask?"

"You've been mopey since the concert. I've never seen you this miserable. Did they do something? Or don't you like my boyfriend?" Madelin hoisted herself onto the counter. "He's not perfect, but he's sweet."

"He's fine." She hadn't given Madelin's boyfriend much thought.

"Was it Mom? She didn't even try to talk to me."

She sighed. "That's a bomb I'm not touching. Your mother has some serious things to work out and you're here because it's a better environment. Trust me, you're better off."

"Ah, that's what I thought." Madelin opened the bag of bread and withdrew two slices. She closed the bag, then tore the slices in half. "She copped to screwing around on Earl?"

"And the things he's been doing to you."

"Oh?" She nibbled on the first piece. "What about David?"

"She wants back with him, but she's not sure how to dump Earl without getting hurt. He's being unkind to her, too and she's afraid that if you're in the house with him, your father will get pissed."

"Dad doesn't want anything to do with me."

"But he also probably doesn't want you to be abused. He thought he was leaving you in a better situation than with him and so far, Earl isn't a better option."

"No." Madelin ate the remainder of the piece, then a second one. "Mom actually thought about me?"

"She is. She's struggling, but she's trying, so give her some credit."

"I will." Madelin tore up the third piece before eating it. "So then it's the guys. What did Martin and Justin do? You seemed to be having fun with them."

"I was."

"Then what? I like them. They're silver foxes." Madelin finished the bread. "Plus, two guys who want to treat you like a princess? Yes, please."

"It's more complicated than that." She wasn't sure how much to explain to her niece. "Trust me."

"I bet it is," Madelin said. "I don't get what you're doing, but I see how they looked at you. It's how David looked at Mom. It's why David keeps going on those long truck routes. He does it to make extra money so Mom isn't struggling."

"I know, but she forgot that."

"She did."

"When it comes to them, it's just that I saw something that made me upset and I don't know how to talk to them about it." This was more than her niece needed to know, but the words came out. "I want to talk to them, but it's..."

"So talk to them. If they like you the way I think they do, they'll appreciate you being honest with them. What'd they do to upset you?"

She drummed her fingers on the counter. "I saw Justin kiss someone else."

"Ouch." Madelin leaned forward. "Are you serious?"

"I'm sure there's more to it than what I saw, but still. It hurt."

"Yeah, it did."

"You're so smart." She shook her head. "How do you know it's killing me?"

"Because I know you and you fell for them. I don't blame you, by the way. I told you, they're hotties, but that's not cool. I'd so call them and ream them out." Madelin left the counter. "Hand them their asses on a plate."

"Platter," she corrected. "I don't want to hand them their asses, but I'd like an explanation."

"Then get one." Madelin handed her the phone. "Now."

"I can't."

"Please," Madelin said. "I've never known you to be this indecisive. And yes, it's one of our vocab words this week and I know what it means. Now call them. I'll be in my room, but I'm expecting you to say things are all smoothed over."

"Thanks." She stared at the phone and debated calling them. If she loved them, then she deserved to know what was going on. Why did that seem so completely difficult?

She picked up the phone and sighed. She had to do this. Had to give them the chance to explain. Without giving herself the opportunity to change her mind, she swiped to Martin's number. As the call connected, she turned and noticed a shadow in front of the window.

"What the hell?" She kept the phone in hand and hurried to the window.

Martin stood on the stoop. No sign of Justin. She disconnected the call and opened the door. "Martin."

"Hi, babe." Martin held a small bouquet of flowers, raggedy at the ends. "For you."

"Thanks." She accepted the daisies. "Where did you get these?"

"The field at the edge of our property."

"You picked wildflowers for me?"

"Justin suggested a spray as big as you are." Martin half-shrugged. "I thought this was better because it's simpler."

"It is." She placed the flowers on the table by the door, then stepped outside. She closed the door behind her. "What are you doing here?"

"Bringing you flowers."

"Oh." She sat on the stoop beside him. "It's been fun being with you." She had to get these words out and make a clean break. The cleaner, the better for everyone involved. Her heart broke, but she had no choice. She wasn't their type. It made the most sense to give them the chance to leave with dignity. A sexy experiment that'd run its course.

"That doesn't sound like the hey, we belong together, I was expecting." Martin stretched out his legs, but crossed his ankles and faced her. "What's going on?"

"I've been thinking about us," she said, forcing herself to speak. "Thinking about what we've been doing and the time together. It's been wonderful. I can't imagine being with anyone else."

"But?"

"But you're both ridiculously wealthy men. I know, because I looked you up online. When I did, I realized it was foolish to get upset that you'd researched me, so for that, I'm sorry. But I looked you up and you're crazy rich. You could have anyone you want, but you're with me. I saw Cindy and she was gorgeous. If she wasn't a model, she should've been. And it hit me. I can't compete with that. I can't be like her or even consider it. I'm never going to be that tall or get rid of these curves. I like to eat and I'm not destined to be thin."

"Chloe."

She held up her hand. "Please. I've practiced this and I need to get through it."

He grasped her fingers, but didn't speak.

"I can't compete with her or your past. I'm not that kind of girl. I've got responsibilities and I can't leave them to have a fantasy life. I wouldn't know what to do with the kind of money you have, the kind of responsibilities you have and I'm not sure I want to. Cindy made me realize I'm out of my league. Then I saw Justin kissing that woman at the concert and my world crashed around me. I'm just one of the women in your life and I can't be among the crowd. When I fall for someone, I want to be the only one. That's not possible with you."

"Who says it's not?"

"Martin." She pulled away from him. "I'm trying to save us all a lot of pain and heartache. I fell for you, but I'm not so foolish to think this will work. It won't, so I'm giving you the chance to go. I'd take the collar off, but I can't." She touched the band of metal around her throat.

"You'll do nothing of the sort." Martin shook his head. "Stop."

"Don't make this harder than it's got to be." Her voice cracked and she bit back a sob. Damn it. Why wasn't he simply letting her go?

"I'll make it as damn difficult as I want because I'm not giving up on you. We're not letting go." Martin reached for her and grasped her hands. "Come here."

She wanted to argue with him, but allowed him to tug her onto his lap. "Martin."

"Listen to me. Will you please do that?"

She nodded, unable to form words. If she tried, she'd cry and she wasn't about to give him that satisfaction.

"The woman you saw on the internet was my wife, yes, but she didn't want to be with both Justin and I.

She refused. She said it was terrible and unnatural. The fact that Justin and I are of the same wavelength and need to share our partner made her sick, so it never would've worked. I loved her, but she only loved me and the piece that was missing always would be."

She didn't understand. Why wouldn't Cindy like them both?

"The woman you saw kissing Justin was one of his exes. She did what she did exactly for the reason you're crying. She wanted him to hurt and you to be humiliated. She wanted to exact pain because she'd been hurt that he'd left her. Just like Cindy, she wasn't interested in being with both of us. She only wanted him and his money. That's not the kind of woman we need in our life."

"No," she whispered. "She's not."

"But you are." He embraced her. "That's why I collared you so fast. That and I didn't want anyone else at the club to take you. You're special."

"I don't understand." They could have anyone.

"We're not easy men to love. Never have been. We want to share our partner and have a triad, which is a huge thing for most people to understand and they don't. You did. You fell right into the rhythm of what we did and didn't blink," he said. "But you're right. I did research you. I did pull strings to get into your orbit after the club. Hell, at the club, we ensured no one else would approach you so we could dance with you. That's the bastards we are — we love to be in charge. I don't regret researching you because it allowed me to understand some things about you long before we had the chance to get to know you. We should've been more upfront with you, but we weren't and I regret that."

She smoothed the wrinkles in his shirt. He'd given her too much to think about and wade through. The idea they'd orchestrated so much bothered her, but it also showed her they cared enough to protect her.

"Cindy would never have been the right woman for us, but she taught me that I could love again. Justin realized finding the one to make our triad whole isn't easy. Once we both understood those facts, we knew we'd have to look harder for our third. When we met you, we knew. It wasn't a lightning strike, but rather a gut feeling. You're the curvy woman of our fantasies and dreams. You've also shown us that a family, no matter what shape and size is possible. We love you and we love Madelin. The concert was so much fun because we were all relaxed. Like that's what we should've always been doing."

She wasn't sure what to say. His words were so right and she wanted to give everything over to them. Sure, they'd done some things that didn't sit well with her, but the reasons were solid. This wasn't done out of malice, but protection.

"I know it's a school night, but we wanted you and Madelin to come over to the house. We've got dinner being prepared. It's not formal and I don't expect anything. Just give us the chance to make this night something special." Martin let go of her hand and caressed her cheek. "I love you, Chloe. I never thought I'd love anyone again, but when we met you, I knew. I realize it'll take time for you to love us, but I know it's possible. Come over tonight, please?"

She couldn't tell him no because she didn't have it in her. "I need to talk to Madelin."

"I figured you did, but I'll wait." Martin brushed his thumb across her bottom lip. "I'm sorry I pushed you, but I'm not sorry I've been as honest as I can."

"I know." He loved her and if he did, then Justin did, too. Knowing that was a dream come true. She left his lap and forced herself into the apartment. She still didn't believe she was the right woman for them, but if they loved her and they saw a future with her, then she'd go on this ride. She wobbled down to Madelin's room. "Hey."

"Hey." Madelin turned her phone over, face down on the bed. "You're back."

"Was I supposed to go somewhere?" She leaned on the doorframe for support. "What are you doing?"

Madelin sighed and her shoulders sagged. "I was chatting with Key. I wasn't sure you'd approve, so we were keeping it on the D-L." She turned her phone back over and the screen was dark. "I guess he left." She swiped back to the lock screen, then to the chat screen.

"Is he gone?"

"He must've bolted when I turned the phone over." Madelin rubbed her forehead. "I screw everything up."

"How?" She didn't have a lot of time, but this needed to be handled. "What'd you do?"

"I get freaked out and nervous, then act and it's not right." Madelin swiped to the chat screen. "See? He jetted."

"So send him a text and explain what happened."

"What?" Madelin tapped the screen. "What do I tell him?"

"The truth. You got interrupted and didn't mean to hang up on him. It's okay." She sat on the bed. "If he really likes you, he'll understand."

"Then why doesn't Mom?"

Oh boy. "What? Where'd this come from?"

"I tried to call her and she hung up on me. She said she doesn't have a daughter and I need to leave her alone."

She couldn't be sure, but she had a pretty good idea what was going on. "I don't know for certain, but I'm guessing she said it because Earl was around. She was trying to keep you safe and keep you out of his line of fire. She's doing her best, okay?"

"She's not disgusted with me?"

"No." She brushed a couple strands of hair from Madelin's face. "It's a fucked-up mess, but she's doing what she can to protect you. You're safe here with me and when things settle down, it'll make a lot more sense."

"Okay." Madelin sighed, then brightened. "He's not mad."

"See?" Her heart broke for her niece. The kid was going through so much more than she should have to. "Your mom is a complicated person. She's had a lot handed to her and didn't have to deal with it. But she's gotten herself into a situation that she's got to figure out all on her own. She will, but it'll take time. You're collateral damage in a way, but you've got the best chance right now because you're out of the fray and you're here where you can be yourself."

"Okay." Madelin offered a weak smile. "What'd you come in here for?"

She'd almost forgotten. "I wanted to invite you to supper. We've been invited to have dinner at Martin and Justin's house."

"We?" Madelin's eyes lit up. "I'm invited, too?"

"Why not?"

"I'm the extra?"

"No. You're my niece, but you're my favorite and you're family. If they're going to be family at some point, then this is a good next step." She offered her hand. "Grab your phone and we'll go. It'll be a good time and we get to see a huge house."

"Mansion?"

"Pretty much." She grasped Madelin's hand. "Come on."

"Yeah." Madelin tucked her phone in her back pocket.

When she rounded the hallway into the living room, Martin stood in the middle of the room. "Hey."

"Hi." Martin grinned. "I'd love to take two beautiful ladies to supper. Are you game?"

Madelin squeezed Chloe's hand. "I am."

"I am, too." Chloe relaxed. "Very ready."

Things weren't totally settled, but at least they were going in the right direction. Her needs would be met and she now had the push to demand what she wanted. If Martin and Justin were the men of honor she knew them to be, they'd come through for her.

She had no doubt.

Chapter Sixteen

Martin drove Chloe and Madelin to the house and his heart hammered. He'd fallen head over heels for Chloe and loved the way she took care of Madelin. She had a natural gift with kids and understood them. He, on the other hand, wasn't sure he'd have ever been a decent dad. He was too involved in his work. The business required too much of him. Kids needed parents who weren't that immersed in their job.

When he arrived at the house he shared with Justin, Madelin gasped.

"Wait. You live here?" Madelin leaned forward in the seat. "This isn't even a real house."

"It's real." He should know. With Justin's help, he'd paid for it, renovated the property and made it their sanctuary. "Would you believe we bought the property for about fifty grand and there was a house already on it, but the house was falling in, so we had it knocked down and built this one?"

"Nuh-uh." Madelin sat back. "You didn't."

"That's his job—to build houses and fix them up," Chloe said. "So yeah, he and Justin probably did those things."

"What was wrong with the house? It was really falling in?" Madelin asked. "You couldn't bring it back to life?"

"Trust me." He parked in front of the garage. "I wanted to. The house had beautiful gingerbread details and the kind of porch I love."

"You could sit on it and not get sunburned?" Madelin asked. "I don't know what gingerbread details are, but they sound interesting."

"Think the pretty curly Qs and decorative overhangs on houses. I'll show you," Chloe said and swiped her phone. "See?"

"Oh." Madelin shrugged. "But I like those porches, too. I've always wanted to sit on one with a swing."

"Well, you can do that here." Martin left the car first. "The back patio has an overhang and I've got a swing out there. I wanted it to be like a whole extra room outside."

"Can I see it?" Madelin asked. "Please?"

"Sure." He ushered Madelin and Chloe into the house. The scent of garlic and freshly baked bread filled the air. "Justin?"

Justin waved from the kitchen. "I'm almost done. Just has to cool for a few minutes."

"Our Madelin wants to see the back patio." Martin nodded to the French doors. "Want to give her a tour?"

"Sure!" Justin waved to Madelin. "Want to see the swing? There's a whole entertainment center out there, too."

"You're kidding." Madelin hurried with him out the door, leaving Martin alone with Chloe.

"So." Martin kicked out of his shoes.

"So." She laced her fingers together. "Thanks for including her."

"You don't have to be so kind or on tenterhooks with me." Martin embraced her. "I wasn't kidding about what I said. I love you. Justin loves you. We didn't collar you for no reason. We did it because we want you in our life. That collar shows you that we care and are devoted to you, too."

The corner of her mouth quirked and she stared at him. "I know."

"So don't think we don't love you."

"I don't think that." She smoothed her hands over his chest. "I think this has all been complicated and you've been too kind about it. I keep expecting you to yell at me. To get angry and use your money or power over me. To lose your patience with me. You're too patient and accepting. I push you away and you take me back. You don't blink. Either of you."

"When you really care about someone, you take the time to understand them and find out what makes them who they are. That's what I've done with you because I care. I want you in my life and if that means being patient, then that's what I'll do."

"I appreciate it." She sighed. "Makes me realize you do care and that I'm in good hands."

"You are," he said. "The things with Cindy and Aline weren't anything for you to worry about. We're just as devoted to you as we hope you are to us."

"I am."

"And one of these days, I want you to show us," he murmured. "You know how."

"I do." She kissed him, then tensed. "I hear them."

"Justin won't care. He'll want to join in."

"Madelin doesn't need to see us like this." She backed out of his arms. "It's not right."

"To see people who love each other embrace and treat each other with respect?" He rubbed her back. "I know. Not pawing each other."

"Yes."

"You're right." He'd try to get in a few more touches later. He and Justin had all the time in the world with Chloe.

Madelin rushed into the room first. She brushed her hair back and her eyes flashed. "Oh my God. Did you know there's a TV out there? Any channel you could want."

"I did," Martin said. He laughed and continued to rub Chloe's back. "I had it installed."

"And I programmed it." Justin carried a bowl of salad out of the kitchen. "It's ready. All I've got to do is bring it to the table. Have a seat and I'll get drinks."

Martin led them to the adjacent dining room. Having Chloe and Madelin in their home pleased him. Like the family he and Justin always deserved. The one they should've had all along. He'd enjoy this as long as it lasted. Chloe was definitely their girl and he'd take any complication that came with her because she mattered.

* * * *

Three hours later, Martin left the apartment after dropping Chloe and Madelin off and his heart lightened. The night couldn't have gone better. He'd made headway with Chloe and even had a few plans for what could be their future. He wanted her moved in as soon as she felt ready and for playtime whenever any of them desired.

When he pulled into the driveway of his house, his phone lit up. Instead of answering, he waited until he'd parked in the garage and checked the screen. He didn't know the number, but few people had his personal number.

"Hello?"

"Hi."

He paused. "Madelin?"

"Sorry. I didn't know if I should call you but I got your number from Auntie Chloe's phone," Madelin said. "You made her really happy today. You and Justin. Thank you."

"You're welcome." He wasn't sure why she'd called, but he liked having a moment to speak to her. "She's been through a lot, hasn't she?"

"She has. She tries to keep it all on the D-L, but it's obvious she's been sad. You guys make her happy."

"I'm glad we do." He paused. "Is that why you called?"

"I called because I wanted to ask you something."

"Okay." He remained in the car. "What's up?"

"Are you going to marry my aunt?"

Well, fuck. He hadn't expected that. He'd thought she'd ask a question about life or sex. "I don't know. Does she want to marry me?" He wasn't even sure which of them Chloe should marry if the situation happened.

"I don't know, but it'd make her happy. She doesn't know I'm calling you and I don't want her to know so she doesn't get angry. Don't tell her, okay?"

"I won't."

"Anyway, you should marry her. She's a catch," Madelin said. "Shit. Gotta go." She hung up and left him in silence.

He sighed and tucked the phone into his pocket. The fact that Madelin felt comfortable enough to call him made him happy. She might have called Justin, too, and that made him happy. He'd made the right decision when he'd met Chloe. She'd given him more than he could ever ask for—a chance at a family of sorts, permanence and the kind of love he and Justin deserved.

Soon, he and Justin would have Chloe with them all the time. If Madelin came along for the family ride, then perfect. He'd do his best to be a parental figure.

Chloe mattered that much.

* * * *

Friday night, Martin finished up the last of the paperwork. When he looked up, Justin walked into the office. He pushed the tablet away and rolled backward in his chair.

"Hey." Justin sat across from the desk. "We're going to the game?"

"I'd planned on it and you look like you're ready to go. You brought extra clothes this morning?" He hadn't seen a bag or anything, but hadn't paid much attention. As for that morning, he'd purchased season passes for him, Justin and Chloe, then made a donation to the school. Having the name of the business on banners at the field hadn't been in his plans until a short time ago, but now he rather liked the idea. Besides, he wanted to help make the band better. If his money could do that, then perfect.

"We're picking Chloe up?" Justin folded his hands across his flat belly and crossed his legs. "I have a surprise for her, if you're up for it."

"Oh?" He'd like to hear this.

"I found some silky soft rope and I thought maybe we could have a quick scene before we left. Madelin wouldn't be there, so no interruptions," Justin said. "We'd use the rope on her, bind her enough for her to feel bound, but not inhibit movement. She'll know she belongs to us, but no one else can see it."

"I like it." He nodded. "She'll have to agree."

"Of course."

"I've been thinking about tonight, too." He shifted in his seat and stared at Justin. "I want to start the contract with her."

"You do?" Justin's brows rose. "I like that."

"I want to make this permanent," he said. "I got a call Wednesday from Madelin and she wants us to get married."

"You and Chloe?"

"Yeah." He chuckled and crossed his ankles. "I never thought I'd want to get married again to anyone. Just be free and happy and do what I wanted."

"She made you change your mind?"

"She's making a strong case that marriage isn't bad. What about you? Have you thought about it?"

Justin tented his fingers and pressed his mouth to his index digits. "I have. When you got married to Cindy, I was so jealous and I wanted to be part of that but she didn't want me."

"Is that why you proposed to Molly?" He'd wondered about his cousin's spur-of-the-moment engagement.

"I never actually proposed," Justin said. "I saw how happy you were, but also how the things we did went away. That's when I saw the unhappiness. I never said anything because I thought that's what you wanted — her."

"I did, but I couldn't get past that need."

"What makes you think she'll want to marry you or me? What if she wants to be free?" Justin asked. "Or just collared?"

"I doubt that. I get the feeling she's yearning to have permanence, too. I don't know if she can legally marry both of us, but what if we could have a civil union that way? What if she has to legally marry one of us, but the civil version means she can have both and we all get what we want?"

"You've thought a lot about this."

"I have."

Justin pressed his mouth to his fingers again. "Ideally, I'd like to have her input before we make a decision, but to be honest, I've thought about this, too. I can't imagine not having her here."

He said nothing, but liked what he'd heard.

"I've also been thinking about the situation here. I'd like her to live with us. I don't expect control outside of the bedroom, but I'd like to make the relationship permanent," Justin said. "After my breakdown at the pond, I've been reassessing my life. I don't want to continue the same shit my father did to me or to my mother. If we settle down, then we do for good. We make it work. I can't hurt her the way I was hurt. I won't."

"I know you won't." He knew his cousin had been abused, but not to the degree. The more he got Justin to talk, the more Justin's hesitancy made sense.

"I thought we'd give her something at the game to signify our devotion to her." Justin sat up, then rummaged in his pocket. "It's not a guarantee of marriage, but to my way of thinking, a guarantee that we're hers forever. She's got the collar, but this is something else."

"I like what you're saying. What are you thinking?" He leaned forward and rested his elbows on the desk. "I'm assuming you've selected something."

"I did." Justin produced a box and opened it. Nestled in the black velvet was a ring. The green stones glittered among the darkness. "This is three emeralds together, outlined with diamonds on a platinum band. I couldn't go cheap on this, but it signifies the three of us together and the circle around the main stones shows we're never ending."

He liked it a lot. "You've got good taste."

"Thanks." Justin closed the box. "I thought we'd give it to her tonight. I can't wait any longer."

"I'm in agreement." He closed his laptop, then stood. "I've got a change of clothes here so we can leave here before heading to her apartment. She texted me that Madelin is already at the school. I guess there was a dance right after school that kept her there."

"Dancing with her boyfriend?"

"I'd assume so."

"I hope she's being safe."

He stared at his cousin. Madelin wasn't their daughter, but he liked Justin's protectiveness. "You talk like a dad." He left his desk, then ducked into the adjacent bathroom to change. He unbuttoned his dress shirt, then shrugged out of it.

"I never thought I wanted to be," Justin said. "I'm not much of a kid person, but she's a nice girl. She deserves to be spoiled a little."

"She does." He switched into a pullover and unzipped his trousers. He stepped out of the pants, then hung those over the rail before switching into jeans.

"I also thought I wasn't ever going to be a parent. I didn't want to settle down and I've been very careful about my sex life," Justin said. "So the idea of having a kid didn't cross my mind. But spending time with Chloe and Madelin makes me wish I hadn't eschewed the notion."

"I get it." He zipped before leaving the bathroom. "She's a great kid."

"And Chloe's the best woman we could've ever asked for."

He located his loafers and collected his phone, wallet and keys. He stepped into the footwear. "I'm ready when you are."

"Then let's go." Justin waited by the door. "I've already locked up the front and set the alarm. My office is locked and that alarm set as well."

Martin flipped the handle on the door leading into his office, then engaged the alarm on his phone before leaving his space. He checked the outer door to be sure it was locked before heading to the truck. Once Chloe mentioned she liked the truck because the bench seat allowed them all to sit together, he'd taken to driving it every time he went to see her.

"I've got the special rope, too." Justin settled on the passenger seat. "We need to keep moving, though, so we're not late. I want to catch pregame."

"I do, too. I hear the band has a new song they're playing tonight." He drove across town to Chloe's apartment. Every mile closer, his spirit lifted. Being with Chloe made him happy.

He parked across from her car in the visitor spaces. In seconds, he and Justin strode up to her front door.

Chloe opened before they could knock and her smile warmed Martin's heart. "Hi." She grinned and stepped away from the door. "Come in."

Like they had to be told? Martin surged into the apartment first and snagged her in his embrace. He kissed her, pushing the connection immediately and sucking on her tongue. She renewed his spirit. When he finally broke the kiss, he stood her on her feet.

"Hi." A dazed look filled her eyes and her smile softened.

Justin gathered her in his arms and kissed her. "I can't match that passion. He's on fire." He rested his forehead on hers. "But I can increase your desire."

"You can?" she asked.

"Uh-huh." Martin sat on the arm of the chair and folded his arms. "Undress."

"Now?" Her eyes flashed. "I..."

"Only to your bra. Panties off. Everything else off." Justin withdrew the length of rope from his pocket. "Girl?"

Her lips parted and she whimpered, then complied. She undressed to only her bra and socks. If Martin wasn't mistaken, her liquid excitement glittered on her shaved pussy. *Hot damn.*

Justin trailed the rope over her chest. "We wanted to make sure you know you're in our care, our bonds, and we've always got you." He draped the rope around the back of her neck, leaving the ends to fall between her breasts. While Martin watched, Justin intricately bound her in the rope, careful to slightly bind her breasts, and tugged on the length between her legs. "No one will know you're bound, and you've got freedom of movement."

"We know you're bound," Martin said. "And it's fucking hot, girl."

"Very." Justin knotted the rope, then stepped back. "Get dressed. It's time to go to a game."

"Yes, sirs." She wobbled, but complied.

Martin drank in the view of her and his desires for Chloe cemented. She'd been made for them and he refused to let her go. After tonight, she'd be theirs forever.

Their curvy, perfect girl.

Chapter Seventeen

Chloe dressed in a hurry, but each time she brushed against the rope, she remembered their touch on her body. She remembered that they owned her. Boy, it felt good.

"Before we go, we need to discuss something." Martin helped her into her jacket. "We'd like to write a contract for the three of us."

"Contract?" Like, to be theirs? She tamped down her excitement, just in case that wasn't what they meant.

"Yes." Justin nodded once. "We've played and we'd like to continue playing with you. We'd like a contract with you that you'll only play with us and that you belong to us. You trust us to give you pleasure and make you fly, but in return we trust you to keep us in check and to let us know that you're happy. To be honest enough to tell us what you want. What you need."

"And...we'll write this all up," Martin said. "Nothing is concrete yet, but we'd like this. What do you think?"

She didn't have to consider their offer for long. Sure, she wanted the wording sorted out, but she'd wanted this all along. "Yes."

"Yes?" Justin tipped his head. "Babe?"

"Yes." She nodded and grasped their hands. "We should knock out the exact wording, but I don't care what it says, to be honest. I know how I feel and how you both feel. I know this is where we're supposed to take this relationship and I'm not afraid." *Not at all.*

"No?" Martin kissed her. "I'm glad."

"So am I." Justin winked, then squeezed her hand. "This is the right step."

"It is," she said. "But we do need to keep moving because unless you've got a parking pass, we're going to have to leave to get a decent spot. I hate parking way out in the field."

"Oh, I've got that under control." Martin held the door for her. Justin exited first, then she did and Martin closed the door behind them. "I donated money to the school for the band program and bought us all season passes as well as a parking pass."

"You did?" She locked up, then faced them. "You didn't have to do that."

"No, but we take care of those we love and we love you and Madelin," Justin said. "Besides, it's doing good for the school, which means it's helping Mad. That's enough for me."

"That's it." Martin walked with her to the truck. "You're our family now and that means she is too, by extension."

Chloe climbed into the truck, but the world seemed to go by in a blur. The knowledge that Martin and Justin wanted her as their toy, but also their girl, overwhelmed her. Then they'd added in caring about her and her niece like family and she wasn't sure what to think. The joy in her heart was more than she could handle. She'd never been the center of attention or the one to have these sorts of things happen to her.

Then she'd met Martin and Justin.

So they'd pushed and orchestrated. So they were a bit forthright for her taste. They weren't always that way. They could be tender and sweet. She shifted and the rope tugged lightly. She bit back a moan. Martin and Justin could also be decadent and naughty — like binding her as she went out in public. The very notion they'd used the rope and made the evening a scene that only the three of them knew about was so dangerously naughty that she loved it.

Justin drove them to the football stadium and parked in the sponsor area. He placed the tag on the rearview mirror, then nodded. "We're legal now."

"And I've got the passes on my phone." Martin left the truck first and held his hand out to Chloe. "How do you feel, babe?"

"Overwhelmed." She slid out of the vehicle and into his arms. "Like I've got a huge secret only I know about and I don't want to share it, but it's almost too big to keep quiet."

"Yeah?" He swatted her ass. "The binding? Or the coupling?"

"Being with you both and having this harness of sorts on me. I love it and I love you, both, too." There. She'd said it. No take backs.

"You do?" Martin swept her off her feet and swung her around twice. "You've made me the happiest man in the world."

"Hey, hey." Justin joined them. "What's the cause for celebration?"

Martin placed her on her feet and she turned, albeit a bit dizzily, to Justin. "I told Martin what I'm going to tell you. I love you. I love him and I love you."

"Hot damn." Justin whooped, then threw his arms around her. "Best night ever and it's barely started."

"Yes." She linked arms with them and allowed both men to take her up to the stadium gates. Martin showed the passes and got them into the facility. She swore she was swept up in the moment, but who could argue? Not her.

"Where does the band come in?" Justin asked. "Is there a special place to sit?"

"The home side, for one." She pointed to the bleachers. "The band is down on the field on those rickety seats, but we can go up here. After the pregame festivities and the actual game starts, the band will sit there, but they'll have freedom for the third quarter."

"Sounds good." Martin gestured to one of the benches. "Will this work?"

"We'll be able to see the band march in from here." She pointed to the far gate. "They come through there, then make their way around the track until they stop in front of us to play a couple songs. After that, they use a quick cadence to get to the far side of the field to line up for pregame."

"You know a lot about this." Justin slipped his arm around her. "It's kind of sexy."

"I try. She's my niece and it makes sense to pay attention, plus, I love football." Not so much high school ball, but whatever. She swept her gaze around the crowd and noticed her sister sitting with David on the other section of the bleachers. She caught her sister's gaze and nodded once. Melinda offered a weak smile, but didn't otherwise react.

Before she could decide if she wanted to walk over to her sister, she heard the band. "Get ready," she said and clapped to the beat. The marching band came into the stadium and the crowd rose to their feet. The sheer excitement of the night amped up. She bit back a whoop. The rope added to her excitement. She was doing something no one else knew about. She applauded as the band marched around the track then stopped in front of the home bleachers. They played a few songs before marching quick time to the ends of the field. Tears blurred her vision as she watched her niece march across the turf.

"She's good." Martin patted Chloe's ass. "Proud of you."

She hadn't done much but give Madelin some grounding.

After the pregame festivities concluded and the football contest began, she patted both Martin and Justin on the thighs. "I'll be right back. My sister is here and I should speak to her."

"Go get 'em, babe." Justin winked.

She left her men and made her way over to the other side of the bleachers. Her sister tensed as she sat down beside her. "Hi."

"Hi." Melinda balled her hands.

"Hi," she said to David. "Good to see you."

David blushed. "I'm sorry I've been away so long."

"That happens." She turned her attention to her sister. "So, are you okay? I see the change. How do you feel?"

"I'm good. I got a restraining order against Earl and had him thrown out. Before I got the order, I called David and confessed everything. I don't know why he took me back, but he did and we're getting this on the right foot. I'd like her to come home eventually. Not for good yet, because I want it to be sorted out, but I want my kid."

"If she wants to, then she can." She wasn't going to hold her niece back. "I'm always available if it gets bad again."

"I know, and I appreciate it. You saved us both." Melinda brushed away a tear. "I screwed a lot up and I'm sorry. I'm sorry I let it all go to hell and wasn't the mom she needed."

"You are now." She hugged her sister. "I'm glad you got the restraining order. He needed to be put in his place."

"He did." Melinda sighed. "David and I had a long talk and it wasn't pretty."

"I don't suppose it was. You're good, though?" she asked.

"We're getting there." Melinda nodded and her chin quivered. "It's smoothing out."

"Then that's what matters." She patted her sister's thigh. "I want you to meet the guys. Are you interested?"

"The guys?" Melinda glanced over at David. "Who?"

"My boyfriends." Chloe sucked in a ragged breath. "I know it's not what everyone else does, but it's what I do. Martin and Justin are good to me."

"I'd like to meet them. Do you?" Melinda asked David.

"Sure." David stood first, then gestured to them. "I'm game."

She left the row, then headed to where Justin and Martin waited. When she neared them, she grinned. "Hey. This is my sister, Melinda and her husband,

David. This is Martin and this is Justin, my boyfriends."
She held her breath as she waited for everyone to meet.

"Good to put a face to a name," Martin said. He
shook hands with David then hugged Melinda. "Nice
to meet you."

"Yes," Justin said and mimicked Martin's actions.
"Have a seat."

"Thanks." Melinda sat beside Chloe. "They're cute,"
she whispered. "You nabbed them both?"

"It's a long story, but yeah." She held Martin's hand.

"You do know who they are? They're like
bazillionaires," Melinda said right against Chloe's ear.
"Building magnates or something."

"I guess, but they're just Martin and Justin to me."
She sighed. "That's what matters."

"It does." She turned her attention to the game. So
far, everyone was getting along. Things seemed to be
going in the right direction.

* * * *

At the end of the halftime show, when the game
resumed, Chloe, along with Martin, Justin, Melinda
and David, made their way to the fencing around the
track. Madelin bounced up to them and hugged her
mother. Although Chloe wanted to get in the mix, she
held back. This moment had to happen between her
sister and niece.

"It'll be okay," Martin murmured. "Don't sweat it."

"I know." Chloe bit back her twinge of jealousy.
She'd worked so hard to get Madelin on the right track
and now she had to stand aside to watch if her efforts
had paid off.

A moment later, Madelin rushed over to them. "I'm so glad you're here." She hugged Chloe, then Martin and Justin. "I didn't think you'd come."

"Why not? I wouldn't miss this for the world." She brushed invisible lint off Madeline's uniform. "How are you feeling?"

"I'm good." Madelin nudged her aside. "I'm glad Mom and David came. I didn't think they'd be here, so it's good to see them."

"Good." She waited a beat. "There's more, isn't there?"

"She wants me to come home for the night tonight. Just a try." Madelin picked at the zipper of her uniform. "I kind of want to, but I don't."

"It's one night and she is your mother. If you want to try, then try. I'll keep my phone on all night in case you change your mind."

"You will?" Madelin's shoulders sagged. "Thank you. I didn't want to hurt you if I said I wanted to give it a shot, but I also didn't want to go and it'd be a disaster."

"I know. You'll be fine, but I'm here if it's not." She hugged her niece, then let go. "Are you going to have her pick you up?"

"Yeah. I've got my stuff in my bag, but I'm coming home in the morning." Madelin nodded. "I won't be gone long."

"Have fun." She waved, then gave the family space.

Having the empty nest of sorts wasn't fun, but she'd manage. As she watched Madelin walk away, she knew she'd made the right choice in giving her freedom. So far, Madelin hadn't decided to return to her mother, but she wanted to spend more time with her.

"It'll be okay." Martin threaded his arm around her. "It's a new beginning, but just the start. It's not forever."

"I know." She leaned into him. "Feels sort of permanent, though."

"It's not." Justin also slipped his arm around her.

"I offered to help and it was used, but things changed. I guess everyone's happy," she said. "We should leave them alone."

"You do know, this means we can have some time together tonight," Martin said against her ear. "Can have a scene and play more with that rope."

"We could." Her body warmed and her desire rose. "And work on that contract?"

"Among other things that are a little more exciting." Justin turned her away from the general crowd. "We wanted to give this to you and there's no time like right now." He opened a little box and presented her with the item.

"This is our token to you that we're not going anywhere. You're ours, yes, but we're also yours," Martin said. "When you look at these gems, you'll see the three of us and know we're forever."

She gasped and stared at the ring. Three emeralds and diamonds surrounding them. She allowed Justin to put the jewelry on her finger. "Wow."

"Will you accept us as your partners and the ones who will give you whatever you need? We're here to build you up, but also stand beside you. Our girl and our treasure," Martin said. "Will you accept us?"

"To give you the best feelings, to make you fly and to use you in ways you never thought were possible, but also to challenge us to be the best men we can be? To make us the men we were always meant to be?"

She marveled at the weight of the jewelry and the sheer beauty. This was more than a token. Good Lord. This was beyond her wildest expectations. She tried to speak, but the words were gone.

"I think we stunned her," Justin said and embraced her. "That's okay."

"We don't mind. When you're ready, we're ready." Martin embraced her, too. "We're not quitting on you."

"I know you're not." She basked in their collective hug. With them, she felt safe. Cherished. "I love it and I accept both of you."

"Then let's take you home and enjoy the gift we've been given in the night alone together and the cementing of the relationship," Martin said. "Yeah?"

"What do you say?" Justin asked.

She watched her niece run off with her friends and her sister leave with her husband. Everyone seemed happy. They'd all gotten the endings they wanted—at least for now. "After the game concludes and I can be sure she's gone home with her mom," she said. "Then I'm all yours." Her heart ached. She'd changed her life for her family and was reaping the benefits of those changes, but still. The separation hurt. A good hurt, though.

"I'm fine with that." Justin kissed her temple.

"Me, too." Martin walked with her from the throng of people. "I know it's a lot to take in, but you're handling it well. You're not alone because we've got you."

"I know." She leaned into Martin and basked in his strength. He was right—she wasn't alone. She'd opened her life up to new experiences and people. Meeting Justin and Martin had been a stroke of luck, but getting closer to her niece had been a saving grace.

She sat with her men through the rest of the game and cheered as the home team won. She applauded the band as they marched past and played for the post game celebrations. When the band marched away, back to the school, Chloe turned to Martin, then Justin. She played with the ring. "I'm ready."

"Yeah?" Martin stood and helped her to her feet.

"I am." She kissed him, then kissed Justin. "I'm ready, sirs. I don't want to use my safe word, but I do have one request tonight."

"Just one?" Justin's brows rose, but he grinned. "What?"

"I want to play at my home," she said. "That way if I do need to get Mad, I know. Or if she comes back to the apartment, it's not empty." Maybe it was irrational to ask this of them, but she had to try.

"Of course." Martin opened the truck door for her. "Family always comes first. You're our family and you're our main concern. Whatever makes you happy."

"Thank you." She climbed into the truck. The rope tugged between her legs and tightened against her breasts. A groan escaped her lips. She'd never make it home and she couldn't wait. She'd have the time of her life tonight.

Let the festivities begin.

Chapter Eighteen

Justin sat in the truck with her and thought about what they could kink out at her apartment. He'd never been in her bedroom and wasn't sure what she might have. Normally, he allowed Martin to run the scene, but he needed to have a bit more control now. Some rules needed to be set before they could have a good time.

He parked in one of the visitor spots, then allowed his cousin and Chloe to leave the vehicle first. Once he locked the truck, he headed into the apartment with them. Excitement filled his head. His skin tingled as he thought about holding her. He'd given her the ring and she'd accepted. She was theirs and life couldn't get much better. It was going in the right direction. He'd found balance and happiness.

Once he stepped into the apartment, Martin wrapped her in a kiss.

Not wanting to be left out, Justin kicked the door shut and pounced. He helped her out of her shirt and kissed her bare skin. Within seconds, he had her down to her bra and the rope. "Gorgeous," he murmured.

Martin untied the rope. As she turned, helping him with the act, Justin pinched her nipple. "Still want to play?" Justin asked. "My love?"

"I do, sirs." She whimpered. "I don't want to use my safe word."

Martin finished untying the rope and let it fall to the floor. "On the bed. Show us your ass."

"Yes, sir." She scampered down the hallway to the bedroom. Once there, she crawled onto the bed and rested on her hands and knees. She waved her ass at Justin and Martin.

Justin bit back a gasp. She had a beautiful body. He admired her curves and her free spirit. "Where are your toys?"

She blushed. "My toys?"

"Naughty girl. I know you have toys," Martin said. "Where are they?"

Justin stood beside his cousin. He rather liked tag-teaming the control aspect. "Girl?"

"My closet. Top shelf." She glanced over her shoulder. "I have been naughty. I've wanted you all night and wanted you to take me to the parking lot to fuck me."

"Did you?" Justin located the box. He opened the lid. Good God, she had quite the collection. He withdrew a vibrator and twisted the cap. The vibration shot through his arm. Damn, the thing had some power.

"What do you want us to do?" Martin asked.

Justin handed him the toy, then withdrew a bottle of lube. Thank God she had the lube. Now they could both be inside her and feel her delectable body. They'd have the throuple they all deserved.

Martin placed the vibrator between her legs. "What do you want us to do?"

She groaned. "Oh God."

"Tell us." Justin snapped the lid back onto the toy box. "No coming until you tell us."

She whimpered and bowed her head. "Spank me, sirs. Please? I need you to spank me."

"Bad girl." Martin kept the toy against her pussy, vibrating her while he brought his hand down hard on her ass. The blossom of pink formed where his fingers had been.

She clawed at the bedding. "One, sir. May I have another?" She groaned again. "May I have both sirs?"

"Yes." Justin undressed and left his clothes in a pile on the floor. He crawled onto the bed and sat before her. Blood rushed to his cock and it bobbed in front of her. "You know what to do."

"Yes, sir." She sucked him to the back of her throat. At the same time, Martin vibrated her.

Justin felt the buzz from the toy throughout his body and especially in his dick. "Yes." He threaded his left hand into her hair to hold her onto his erection.

While she moved her head, Martin spanked her again. He swatted her in rhythm with her movements.

She writhed and whimpered, but didn't pull away. She seemed to move with gusto instead.

"No, you don't. Not yet." Martin spanked her a fourth time, then stopped. He turned the vibrator off before tossing it onto the bed. "We're not done with you." He backed away from her and undressed.

Justin withdrew from her mouth. "I need that pussy. Come here."

"Yes, sir." She did as told with longing in her eyes.

He reached for her and pulled her onto his lap. When she settled over his cock, he tugged her down onto his shaft. The pressure on his dick turned his insides out. He palmed her breasts. "I love your tits."

She parted her lips and need filled her eyes. "Yeah?"

"Very much." He pinched her nipples, then tugged. When she trembled, he repeated his actions. "Getting close?" God, he was.

"Yes, sir." She shivered and dug her nails into his shoulders. "May I come, sir?"

"Nope." Martin spanked her. "Lean over. I want your ass."

Justin let go of her breasts and enfolded her in his arms. "Good girl," he murmured. "Relax. We want to become one with you."

She pressed her face to his neck. "Yes, sir."

Justin slid one hand between their bodies and caressed her clit. "I loved seeing you tied up. Seeing you horny and craving us."

Martin spanked her once more. "We loved it."

He watched his cousin, but spoke to Chloe to reassure her. "When we saw you at the club, we wanted to bind you in our cuffs and spank you. Hear you cry out our names. Hold you when you're upset and cheer with you when you're happy. See you in the morning and last thing at night. Our girl. Our treasure."

"Yes, our treasure." Martin finished spanking her. He lined himself up with her hole and added more lube. Seeing her like this and so needy spurred him on. He couldn't get enough and wanted her right on the edge.

He was about to tumble right into oblivion.

Christ. She blew his mind.

She trembled harder as he dribbled another squirt of lube on her hole. He'd prepped her as much as he could, but still, he moved slowly.

She shivered harder. "Oh, God, yes. Yes, sirs."

He caressed her puckered skin. The cadence of Justin spanking to her helped add to the moment. They were all one.

He pushed into her ass. He moved slowly, a fraction of an inch at a time, sinking into her. The fullness of both dicks in her body overwhelmed him. This was so perfect and right. He slid into her to the hilt.

"My God." She gasped. "I…"

"Breathe," Justin said. "Relax. We've got you. Just breathe, my love."

"Relax," Martin added as he held on to her hips. "We've got you and won't let anyone hurt you. You're protected."

She clawed at the sheets, but shifted slightly between them. "Yes, sirs. Feels so good. I can't breathe."

Neither could he. Martin growled and squirted a little more lube onto her ass. He needed to move, but wanted to draw this out.

Impossible.

Being inside her blew his thoughts all to hell.

Right now, he needed to get moving. Sliding in and out of her was exactly as he'd expected—sublime. In seconds, he and Justin worked a steady cadence, pushing into her at the same time and nearly pulling out before going right back in.

She writhed between them, her trembles increasing as she buried her face against Justin's neck.

Martin spanked her twice, creating a rosy blush on her ass again.

Her yelp and moan encouraged him.

"Are you on the edge?" Justin asked. "Ready to tip over?"

"Yes," she said and panted. "Please, sirs? May I come, please?"

"Do you like me touching your clit while we fuck you?" Justin asked. "While Martin claims your ass?"

Martin increased his speed. He couldn't think straight. "Fuck, you're pulling me in and not letting me go. You love it."

"Yes." She tensed. "I love you both."

Christ. She'd be his undoing. Being with her like this, the three of them becoming one body and mind moving together. Now that they'd found her, he knew to his core they should've been doing this all along.

This was where they belonged.

Martin lost himself in the sheer thrill of being with her. There were no barriers, no worries, just love and devotion. He'd fallen hard for her.

More than fallen.

He was devoted. She'd be theirs forever because he and Justin refused to let her go. Now that they'd found her, they were complete.

"Come for us," Martin said. He spanked her hard. "Come and let go. Cry out."

"Fuck," she yelped and tensed all over before scratching at Justin's shoulders. Like the coil within her snapped, she relaxed. Her inner walls fluttered around him.

Feeling and hearing her come apart pushed him over the edge. Martin growled. "Fuck."

Justin tipped his head back and groaned. He surged into her before he stilled. "Jesus Christ."

No holding back now. Martin tumbled into the sweet bliss of climax. He added a couple more thrusts before his legs turned to jelly. He leaned over her. "My God, you're beyond measure."

Justin opened his eyes and laughed. "How are you...sentences?"

His cousin made little sense, but he understood. "No clue."

"I can't move," she managed. "Can't think."

Martin's thoughts were a little messed up, too. He eased slowly out of her and collapsed beside her on the bed. He panted and stared at the ceiling, needing a few moments to gather his wits before he tried to make coherent sentences.

She slid onto the bed and sighed between him and Justin. Her breathing and the way she rested her hand on his bare thigh pleased Martin. He loved how she touched him. When she did, he felt the love so strongly, like it was always meant to be.

"You're impossible," Chloe said. "Totally."

"How?" Justin rolled onto his side and smoothed his hand across her belly. "What do you mean?"

Martin said nothing, but listened. The words he wanted to say were gone. Not surprising, being he was still reeling after sex.

"How am I supposed to live without you after this?" she asked. "Nothing will be as good as this."

"Doesn't need to be," Martin said, finally finding his voice. "We'll make it work. That's what we do."

"Even with my various complications?" she asked. "Come on."

"Even with." Martin propped himself up on his elbow and met her gaze. "Sweetheart, you're more than our girlfriend or someone we scene with. You're ours. We've fallen in love with you and that's not going away."

"He's right." Justin tangled his legs with hers. "No relationship is ideal, but we've got a good thing. Eventually, we'll get you moved out of here and into the house, but when you're ready. If that means your niece comes along, then she does. It's okay."

"You're serious?" She shifted her attention between them. "Really?"

"Very much so. You're the most important person in our lives." Martin caressed her chin. "I know it's hard to understand, but it's the truth."

"I believe you." She sighed and closed her eyes. "It's a lot to think about, but I'm glad. I never thought you'd be the one to help me and make me happy, but you have. I'm whole."

"We feel the same." Justin tucked against her. "So we move forward and figure it out."

"We will." She opened her eyes and grinned. "I feel like a princess. Like this is all a dream. I don't know if I deserve it, but I'm not questioning anything. I'm happy and I found my place."

"You have." Martin gazed at the two people who meant more to him than any amount of money or object. His cousin was the other half of his brain and should've been his brother. Chloe was the object of his affection, devotion and heart. He'd never be the same and didn't want to be. She made everything better.

"So we figure this out as we go along, but it's we three?" she asked. "Us three?"

"We three," Justin said. "All the way."

"We will, babe." Martin held her and his life balanced. The future had brightened the second he'd met her and now that he had her in his world for the duration, the possibilities were endless. They'd found the one because they had their curvy girl.

Their curvy goddess.

Sign up for our newsletter and find out about all our romance book releases, eBook sales and promotions, sneak peeks and FREE romance books!

Want to see more from this author?
Here's a taster for you to enjoy!

Club Sixxes: Another Sweet Smile
Wendi Zwaduk

Excerpt

"Somebody come play with me," Onyx Power sang as she stopped at the bar and filled her tray. She sang along with the music on the speaker and paid little attention to the people who'd arrived at the club for the night. She'd come to Sixxes to scene and enjoy her evening, but like too many nights, she'd been roped into working. How could she say no? She owed too many people favors.

God.

"Are you here for the evening?" Sadie asked. She stood next to Onyx and filled her tray with glasses. "I wasn't going to, but they asked and I could use the tips."

Nice. Sadie got tips, while she had to work off debts.

"I am." She poured cola into two of the glasses, then lemon-lime soda into three others before mixing up cherry soda for the remainder. The club encouraged the attendees to drink, but nothing hard. Everyone was subjected to a code of conduct. No drugs, no booze and no illicit acts. If it was illegal or could impair the players without consent, then it was forbidden. She didn't mind. She'd rather everyone have a cool head, rather than be silly drunk or worse. "I wanted to play tonight, but I don't know who I want. It's hard to figure it out. Who will be the right Dom? You know?" She had an idea, but it wasn't the right time to tell anyone she had a preference.

"I do." Sadie finished filling her tray. "There are some high-rollers here tonight. I heard there's a couple pairs of billionaires in the house. Can you imagine? Being snapped up by a billionaire? I'd so make them cover me in furs, diamonds and spoil me rotten. I'd deserve it."

She snorted. Of course Sadie would think she deserved to be spoiled. Sadie wanted everyone to bow to her and see her importance. She might be a sub, but Sadie had a wide dominant streak. If she wanted something, Sadie didn't stop until she got it, so everyone else needed to get out of the way.

Onyx wished she could be so forceful, but she didn't have it in her. Not after what she'd been through. "I need to deliver these drinks."

"You could be delivering to a man dripping with money. Keep that in mind." Sadie elbowed her. "You've got the slave garb on. Did you get a Dom? Or did you finally get a position as a club slave?"

"I just told you I didn't have a Dom, but I'm considered a club slave." She'd opted—not totally of her own volition—to be in service of the club and the Doms there for the evening. At any moment, she could be asked to join a scene and that thrilled her, despite her frustration with her position in life.

"Oh. I guess I missed that." Sadie shrugged, then walked away, leaving her at the bar.

Onyx ensured the tray was clean and that she'd stocked it with napkins, then turned on her heel. Walking around the club in nothing but the collar, cuffs, stockings, garter and heels pleased her. Her breasts swayed and her nipples beaded. A pair of clips with bells would be fun, but only if a Dom presented them to her. She liked being on display. Liked knowing anyone in the club could see her and might even be lusting after her. Might want to play.

For all she knew, her dream man could be there tonight.

She delivered her drinks to the various players, then carried the tray back to the bar. The chilly air swept across her body and her nipples beaded anew. She bit back a moan. She longed to be touched by a lover and Dom, not just the wind. To feel his hands along her ass, spanking her, bringing her pain and pleasure, his fingers swiping across her pussy, smearing her cream over her body and pushing into her with his hot cock.

One day.

"Are you interested in joining a scene?"

She stiffened at the sound of the man's voice. She'd heard this voice before, but never directed at her. She'd dreamed and fantasized about that voice. Part of her barely believed he'd approached her.

Zephyr Anderson. He and his business partner Jinx Collins were two of the richest men in the tri-county area and last she knew, they were single. If one of them wanted to talk to her, then she'd pay attention — even if she barely believed it was true.

She held onto the tray. "Do you need to me to take your drink order?" She smiled and met his gaze. Her hands shook and she gripped the tray. "What would you like?" She must've misheard his question because he couldn't possibly want her to play with them. Maybe he wanted her to perform for him.

That had to be it.

He tipped his head. "I didn't ask for a drink. I asked if you wanted to join a scene."

"Oh." She should put the tray down, but she kept it to hide the trembling in her hands. He'd not only paid her attention, but was asking her for one of her fantasies come to life. She should comply, but she should also answer him. Why weren't her legs working and where were her words?

"Do you want to?" he asked. He tipped his head. "Girl?"

She didn't have the option to say no, not really. She was a house slave and had to cooperate with the Doms. But he was asking her if she wanted to play. Not demanding. Not pressuring. Nothing like any other Dom in the building.

She stared at him. Zephyr Anderson. All six-foot-five inches of him towered over her, even at her own five-foot-nine inches. He always seemed to have bed head, but it worked for him. Tattoos covered his arms and his brown eyes sparkled. She swore a stiff breeze would knock him over. She longed to run her fingers through his hair and hear him say her name. The gravelly sound of his voice always sent shivers down her spine. Was he tattooed all over? Pierced? She wanted to find out. She wanted to kiss him, too. Taste him. Kneel before him and have him pull her hair. She wondered what it'd feel like to have him fuck her. To hear him talk dirty to her and make her beg on her knees.

It'd probably feel like heaven.

What would it feel like to be between him and Jinx? She couldn't even fathom it.

"Girl?" Zephyr took the tray from her. "Do I need to turn you over my knee?"

God, that would be wonderful.

"Well?" Zephyr placed the tray on the closest table. "I can tell you're thinking about it. Maybe you'd like to discuss this in another room? Away from the eyes on you, and the listening ears?"

"I…" At least she'd found her voice. "I'm sorry."

"You're not interested?" He half-smiled. "I understand. It's a lot to be part of a scene when you don't know the players. It's fine."

"No." *Good God*. She massaged her temple. She'd fucked this all up. "I'm sorry." Her cuffs rattled and she pressed her lips together. She was there to serve him, yet she couldn't manage the words, *yes I want to play*. She had to look like a fool.

"Okay. I get it now." He grasped her hand. "Let's go into the other room. We need to talk and I want you to feel a little more at ease. There's a lot of pressure out here and this needs some discussion."

"Sure." She didn't fight him as he led her from the room. She probably should've been on a leash, but whatever. No one had signed a contract with her or collared her. For the evening and so many others, she was property of the club.

Except now she could be his property. What a delicious thought.

She straightened her spine and bowed her head. If he wanted her, then she'd do what he wanted. "Yes, sir."

"So you can talk?" He opened one of the velvet-covered doors and led her into the adjacent room. "Good to hear your voice."

She's spoken to him already, but she understood his frustration. "Sorry, sir." She should explain, when the time was right.

"Are you?" He let go of her and folded his arms. "I've seen you around the club. You're collared, but you're not someone's girl, are you?"

"No." She focused on the carpet. She wasn't supposed to look at him, but damn it, she wanted to. "I'm a club slave."

"I see. Just a moment." Zephyr walked away from her, then opened the door.

To bring in the boss? To have her punished, not in a scene, but for misconduct and non-compliance?

Fuck.

Another man entered the room and she fought the urge to look up at him.

Jinx?

God, she could only dream.

"You got her to come in?"

She pressed her knees together. She knew that voice, too. Jinx was there and discussing her. Holy shit. He was real.

"I did." Zephyr walked around her. "I think it's time we had a discussion, but that's only possible if we're all equals. What do you think?"

"I agree." Jinx curled his fingers under her chin, forcing her to look at him. "What do you think?"

They wanted her opinion? They were treating her like she had a stake in this? She cleared her voice. "I'd like that, if that's what you're offering."

"It is." Jinx caressed her chin, then let go and gestured to the sofa. "Sit."

She hesitated a moment, then settled on the cushion. She kept her spine straight and rested her hands on her knees. Was she on display? If so, then she'd do her best to make them happy.

Jinx dragged a wooden chair over to the sofa and faced her. He turned the chair around and sat across from her.

Zephyr sat beside her on the sofa. "As I said, we've seen you around the club and noticed you're collared by the club, but you're not collared by a Dom. Why is that?"

"I've never been asked." Never been approached for more than a scene here and there, or group play. "I guess I'm not what they're looking for." Not when the Doms found out why she'd been put into service at the club. They didn't want that kind of baggage.

"Why's that?" Jinx rested his arms on the back of the chair.

She forgot about the question and practically drooled over him. He looked every bit a model. He wore his jet-black hair short, almost in a crew cut. He smelled good and smiled easily. Where Zephyr was tall and lanky, Jinx was compact and muscular. He had tattoos all over his arms as well, but he had an air of sophistication about him.

"Girl?" The corners of Jinx's mouth curled in a smile. "What are you thinking?"

She'd been drawn to both men, but never had the gumption to speak to them. This was the time to speak up. "I'm too tall, too thin and I'm not the spunky, cute little subs. I guess they don't want someone who's me." Someone without her baggage or issues. She owed the wrong people too much and it'd be a long time before she paid her debt.

"I see." Zephyr crooked his brow. "I've seen you serving here. You're desperate to play and to be seen, but no one sees you. You help so they'll want you."

He'd read her so well, yet knew nothing. "Yes."

"And you're dying to belong to someone." Zephyr toyed with the shoelaces of his boot. "If you're going to be in a scene with someone like us, what do you like in your scenes? In your play?"

She'd never been asked this way—so plainly—but she had to respond. "I prefer discussion and debate to start."

"During a scene?" Jinx rocked back in his seat, then leaned forward again. "Very well. What are your kinks?"

Was she being interviewed? For a prospective position with them? She had nothing to lose. "I like spanking, toy play, cuffs, exhibition, blindfolds and I like orgasming, but I don't want penetration until I'm fully collared. It probably sounds old-fashioned or ridiculous, but that's what I want. I don't want penetration if it's only for the scene. If I'm going to be penetrated, other than with toys, it should be because the Dom respects me and is only with me." She'd been used a few times and wasn't about to do that again. She hated being a toy, unless that's what was expected from the scene.

She bit back the shudder and fought to bury the memories of that relationship. The past was something she'd rather forget.

"I see," Jinx said. "I respect your honesty."

"I also don't want a bunch of other players, unless you're requesting a voyeurism scene," she said. She realized how the balance of power worked here. She wore nothing, save for the cuffs, collar, garter, stockings and heels, but still. She wasn't about to be pushed around, unless it was in a scene.

"Very well." Zephyr nodded, then scooted closer. "We'd like to have a scene with you, just the two of us, using your kinks. I must ask, though, what you don't want."

"Yes, sir." She folded her hands on her lap. "I should probably be on the floor for this. At your feet?"

"No." Zephyr shook his head. "This isn't the scene, yet. When we do, then we'll discuss what will happen."

Yet. When. The words gave her hope. "I don't get into blood play, knives, needles, gun play, kidnap play, suffocation or breath play. I don't want denigration or whipping. I'd prefer no extra partners in the scene and I don't want my own sub."

"Very well," Zephyr said. "What's your safe word?"

"Pumpkin." It was a silly word, but one not used in scenes. She flattened her hands on her lap. "What should I call you in a scene?"

Zephyr crooked his brow. He dipped his head once, then slid his gaze to Jinx before smiling. "When we play, you will address us both as Sir."

"Yes, Sir." His tone gave her more hope.

"Very well." Jinx nodded to the floor. "Would you like to play, girl? Tell us your safe word once more."

She sucked in a ragged breath. Holy hell, she did want to play. "I would like to, yes, Sir. My safe word is pumpkin, but I don't want to use it."

"On your knees." Zephyr stood. He widened his stance and folded his arms. "You know what to do, girl."

She did. She slid to the floor, then rested on her knees. She bowed her head before clasping her hands together behind her back. If she was ever ready to play, it was now.

She blew out a ragged breath as Zephyr, then Jinx, walked around her. She stuck her chest out to entice them. Not even an hour ago, she hadn't thought she'd be playing tonight. Half an hour ago, she'd sworn Jinx and Zephyr wouldn't want to scene with her.

Now both had come true.

"You've got beautiful breasts," Jinx said. "Just right for my hands." He knelt in front of her and slipped his fingers along one of her tits. He caressed her nipple, rolling and tugging on the tender flesh.

The move ripped a groan from her chest. She loved the pain of a scene. The pain delighted her. She spread her knees and the tingle in her pussy spread through her body. Could they see her cream?

"These need clips. Next time, we're putting something on these to keep them nice and hard." Jinx palmed her other breast, then swatted her tit. "Like that?"

She trembled with joy. "Yes, Sir. Thank you, Sir. May I have another?"

"Not yet." Jinx stood, then stepped back.

Zephyr slipped his fingers into her hair, then tugged her head back. Not yanking, but gentle pushing and forcing her to look at him. She parted her lips. Did he want her mouth open? Want her to prepare to give him oral sex? She'd said no penetration, but if they used a toy, she'd comply.

"You've got beautiful eyes, too." Zephyr leaned over and massaged her scalp. "Stand." He let go of her hair.

She did as he asked and managed to scramble to her feet.

"You like to be spanked?" Zephyr asked.

"I do." She shivered. Would he spank her? "Thank you, Sir. I deserve that punishment." Oh, boy, did she deserve that punishment.

"Then come here." Jinx clipped a leash onto the D-ring on her collar and led her across the room to the St. Andrew's cross. "You know what to do."

She did. She stepped onto the platform and spread her arms. She kept her back to them and bared her ass. A fresh wave of tingles shot through her. She widened her stance. Her skin prickled. Being put on display like this thrilled her. She flexed her toes in her shoes and wished she could press her knees together. If they swiped their fingers across her pussy lips, they'd find out just how much she wanted this.

Wanted them.

Zephyr strode around to the back of the cross and slapped a riding crop on the palm of his hand. "Do you want this?"

"I do, Sir. Thank you, Sir." She flattened her hands on the wood as Jinx clipped the cuffs to the thick rings at the ends of the cross. "May I have a spanking, Sir?"

Jinx trailed his fingers down her spine, then flattened his palm on her ass. The sound echoed in the room and the pain radiated through her body. She moaned, then arched toward another spanking.

"So needy." Zephyr twirled the crop in his fingers. "I believe our girl is ready for us."

Ready was an understatement.

"Tell us your name, girl," Zephyr said. "We need to know who we're playing with."

She had to tell them. "Onyx." She'd fought the urge to use her fake name, Ruby. Why lie when she could be bare and honest?

She wobbled and held onto the cross. The worries in her mind, her concerns and anything else bothering her completely evaporated from her thoughts. They wanted her and they'd get what they wanted.

She'd make them happy.

About the Author

Wendi Zwaduk is a multi-published, award-winning author of more than one-hundred short stories and novels. She's been writing since 2008 and published since 2009. Her stories range from the contemporary and paranormal to BDSM and LGBTQ themes. No matter what the length, her works are always hot, but with a lot of heart. She enjoys giving her characters a second chance at love, no matter what the form. She's been the runner up in the Kink Category at Love Romances Café as well as nominated at the LRC for best contemporary, best ménage and best anthology. Her books have made it to the bestseller lists on Amazon.com and the former AllRomance Ebooks. She also writes under the name of Megan Slayer.

When she's not writing, she spends time with her husband and son as well as three dogs and three cats. She enjoys art, music and racing, but football is her sport of choice.

Wendi loves to hear from readers. You can find her contact information, website details and author profile page at https://www.firstforromance.com

ENTWINED PUBLISHING